RED INDIAN

The Beginning

TERRY FOSS

Terry Foss

Published by: Fossil

4 Harvard Drive

Mount Pearl, Newfoundland and Labrador,

Canada

A1N 2Z7

ISBN 978-0-9940209-4-9

Published July 2017

Printed in United States

Edited by: Julieanne Reddy

Cover Art: Claude Randell

Dedication

This book is dedicated to Shiloh, our gentle husky who faithfully warmed my feet during the winter while I wrote this book. You were deeply loved, sadly missed, and will never be forgotten.

Special thanks to Dale Foss for capturing her likeness so well, on that last day.

The past has a way of reaching up from the basement of time to grasp our hearts and minds, often stirring our conscious to a sense of responsibility that we may not necessarily own.

Preface

This is the third book in the Red Indian series. It follows the family lines of Shanadee and Kirradittii, the primary characters in *The Early Years*, the first book in the series. As you begin to read, you will be taken back to the year 1706 to meet Shanadee's great-great-grandfather. From there you will get to spend time with each generation until you once again meet Nanolute, Shanadee's father, who you briefly met in *The Early Years*. You will then be taken on a similar journey with Kirradittii's family in Part 2 of the book.

Living in a time before pencil and paper the Beothuk preserved their history by relating stories of their ancestors while sitting around their cooking fires. In the pages of this book you will find some of those stories that were repeated by the members of two families, generation after generation.

Terry's Books

Through Beothuk Land

Holmes

Beothuk Slaves

Bloody Point

Red Indian - The Beginning

Red Indian - The Final Days

Red Indian - The Early Years

Part 1

Shanadee's Family Tree

Aboboneek & Shawwayet

Baroodisick & Dattomensh

Haddowaddet & Gaboweete

Nanolute & Manddilleeitt

Shanadee

Chapter 1

1706

Aboboneek lay there contentedly listening to the waves wash up on the sandy seashore, as they tumbled the tiny rounded pebbles that lined the coast and drew them back as the water retreated down the beach again. It was a familiar sound, a sound he had heard ever since he was a small boy. There was something comforting in its repetition. The first rays of daylight were filtering through the smoke hole at the top of the mamateek, pushing back the shadows, heralding the beginning of a new day. All night long the wind had howled, exhausting itself to the point where it could now only manage a few final gasps, barely ruffling the leaves of the overhanging trees. The storm was over. It promised to be a quiet day. He was glad. He stretched his cramped legs underneath the heavy furs.

To his left, he sensed, more than saw, movement in the pre-dawn gloom. It was Baroodisick climbing out of his bed, heading for his mother's. He smiled as he watched his son crawl under the covers and cuddle into Shawwayet.

Three years ago, when Baroodisick was born, life had changed for him and Shawwayet. Most of the couples their age already had children and Shawwayet had been feeling left out, unable to join in with the other women's conversations which inevitably turned to the exploits of their children. That was no longer the case. She was much happier now. She was a part of it and he imagined her stories of their son's achievements rivaled any of the other mothers.

His mind drifted back to the night Baroodisick was born. It had been in the midst of a violent summer storm. Lightning had flashed across the sky, lighting the camp as if it were day, immediately followed by great crashes of thunder that rumbled over the mamateeks, shaking the ground beneath them. It had only seemed appropriate they call him Baroodisick, the word for thunder.

As it turned out, we couldn't have picked a better name for him, he thought. For the first two years all he did was scream and yell. The only good thing to come out of that was that we got to have a mamateek all to ourselves. No one else wanted to stay with us with all that racket.

With a smile, Aboboneek pushed back the covers and stood to his feet. He tossed some wood on the fire, pushed aside the caribou skin, and stepped outside. He glanced down as he felt something nuzzle against his leg. He smiled into the dark eyes of Nordea and his mind wandered back to the day he found her.

It was almost two years ago. He had been hunting alone that day. The worst of the winter had passed, but heavy snow still covered the forest. He'd spotted the single tracks of the moisamadrook (wolf) in the snow and he'd noticed the bloodstains that dotted the trail between the footprints. His first instinct had been to head in the other direction. He'd had no desire to encounter a wounded moisamadrook, especially by himself. He'd pulled an arrow from his quiver and notched it in his hathemay (bow). With his right hand, he felt the handle of his knife at his side, making sure it was loose in case he needed it in a hurry. He'd carefully scanned the woods around him but could see no other animals. His breathing slowed and his muscles were tight with tension. He listened quietly. The only sound was the loud thumping of his heart. It seemed he was alone. He'd turned and looked further down the trail. The blood stains were larger and more frequent. The animal appeared to be dragging at least one of its feet. The signs told him it wouldn't be going much farther. He decided to follow. At least he would get its skin. It would make a nice coat, and an even better story.

As he crept around the next bend in the trail he saw where the animal had veered off the path. He wondered if it knew he was following and he turned and peered into the woods behind him. He didn't want to be surprised by it if it had doubled back, as they were known to do. It didn't seem likely though. The moisamadrook was now dragging its hind quarters, creating a red furrow through the white powder. Squatting in the snow, Aboboneek stared at the base of a thick evergreen tree where the blood trail seemed to end. When his eyes had finally adjusted, he could make out the bloodied gray body of the wounded animal in the tangle of undergrowth. It didn't seem to be moving. He'd watched it for a while and then stood to his feet and slowly approached it with his hathemay at the ready.

He'd tentatively nudged it with his boot. There had been no life remaining. Its back legs and belly were ripped and bleeding. It appeared to have been in a fight it didn't win. He'd rolled it over and found the small pup nuzzled beneath the protective fur of its mother's throat. It couldn't have been more than a few weeks old. She must have carried it in her mouth; he had only seen her tracks in the snow.

He still wasn't sure why, but he had impulsively picked it up by the scruff and dropped it in his side pouch. Maybe it was the newness of the recent birth of his own son that made him do it. Somehow the little pup had stirred his emotions, lying there alone and helpless next to its dead mother.

There had been a fair amount of opposition when he returned to camp, not the least of which came from Shawwayet.

"You're not bringing that thing in here," she'd exclaimed.

"She's harmless. She's only a pup. Look at her."

"She will grow into a full grown moisamadrook some day. She can't be inside the mamateek with us. You have a new baby. That's a wild animal."

There were others in the camp that thought he should just kill it, once they found out he had the pup. Eventually most of them came around, some more reluctantly than others.

It had not been easy, but he had been able to convince Shawwayet to keep it inside for the first few weeks until it had grown enough to be on its own. After that, Nordea lay against the side of the mamateek just outside the door. Anywhere he went she followed close behind his heels.

He reached down and scratched behind her ears as she sat on her haunches and affectionately leaned against his leg. Together they looked out over the camp, surveying the damage the storm had left behind.

Two of the seven tapaithooks (canoes) had been torn from their racks in last night's wind storm and lay on their sides farther down the beach, amongst the sea-washed wood and debris that had been thrown up onto the sand during the night. It looked like one must have been thrown end over end, for both the front and back were stove in. The other had a dried branch sticking out of its side, pierced through by the dead tree where it had come to rest.

"Guess those two will need to be fixed up, or maybe even scrapped" he muttered aloud, to no one in particular. He drew in a deep breath of the salt tinged air, letting it fill his chest, replacing the last of the stale sleep laden air from last night.

Around the camp, others were emerging from their mamateeks. The day was slowly awakening. The routines of camp life were about to begin.

Today, he and the rest of the men from the camp would be joining men from other camps along the river to carry out the annual caribou hunt. They had spent the last few weeks cutting down trees and repairing the caribou fences that ran along the river for about a two-day's journey. It was a lot of work keeping the fences together, but it was also a time to get to see members of the tribe he hadn't seen all winter. Aboboneek loved it. It was the best time of the year. There was the excitement of the caribou running through the fences, but there was also the feeling of community the event always brought with it.

The herds were now on the move, heading for their summer feeding grounds. Members of the tribe in the interior would direct the animals into the run created by the fences and the caribou would begin their trip downriver. Along the way, small box corrals had been built near each band's camp where the caribou could be harvested. No band took more than they needed. When they had their animals, those remaining in the corral were herded back into the run. It was the way of the hunt and ensured everyone had enough.

With their camp located on the coast, Aboboneek and his friends were the last to harvest. With the hundreds of caribou that entered the run each year, there was never a concern of not getting enough animals for the camp.

By midmorning they left the camp, making their way to the caribou run under a cloudless summer sky. There were sixteen of them; most of the men of the camp and some of the older boys. For some of the boys it was their first hunt. Aboboneek remembered his first hunt and the nervous excitement that had gripped him that day. He saw it now in the faces of the boys walking ahead of him. Some of them were talking too much while others were noticeably quiet, lost in their thoughts of what the day would bring for them.

He and Nordea were the last in the line, walking alone. Most were still uncomfortable walking next to a moisamadrook and gave her a respectable distance. Aboboneek didn't mind. He enjoyed her company more anyway.

By the time they reached the start of the fenced run, those ahead in the line had made the decision to enter and follow it to the first corral.

Aboboneek stopped and looked down the run. On both sides, the felled trees formed high impenetrable walls ending at the edge of the river. There was no escape for the stampeding caribou, and here at the end they would be forced into the river by those pushing from behind. It would be easy to take them here in the water, so he was not sure why those at the front had decided to go farther upstream. It would just be farther to carry the animals if they took them at the first corral.

He watched as the last two boys disappeared around the first bend in the run, about an arrow's shot from where he stood. At his side, Nordea lifted her head and sniffed the air expectantly. He saw her ears prick and then he heard the signal drums in the distance, announcing the animals were in the run. As the drums went silent they were replaced with the distant thunder of the racing caribou and he knew the group ahead of him was in trouble. Inside the run the tangle of downed trees muffled the sound and they would not be aware how close the stampede was.

"Let's go," he said urgently to Nordea and broke into a run. He knew he had to warn those ahead of him. With her ears flattened, Nordea loped along beside him staying close to his side.

Just as he'd expected, once he entered the run he could no longer hear the approaching herd. He rounded the bend where he'd last seen the two boys and saw five of them strung out along the run ahead of him.

He began to yell. "Climb the fence. Get out of the way. The caribou are coming." He vigorously waved his arms trying to get their attention.

Finally, the two nearest him turned to see what he was yelling about but the others were too far ahead to hear him and kept going.

Nordea threw her head back and howled.

The lead boy, who was nearing another bend in the Run, stopped, glanced over his shoulder, and then whirled back in alarm to face the tightly packed charging caribou that suddenly appeared in front of him.

Too late, he turned to run but was quickly overtaken and disappeared underneath the racing hooves of the panicked animals. The other two managed to get to the wall and began to climb the tangle of trees.

The one on the left found an opening and dived through as the rushing herd rushed by. The one on the right had only begun to climb when one of the caribou knocked him from his perch as it raced by. Aboboneek watched helplessly as he bounced from its back and tumbled out of sight.

The closest boys had found holes in the fence and had managed to crawl through to safety. He turned to Nordea and yelled "run," as he grabbed the limbs of the nearest trees and scrambled up the wall to escape the stampede that was bearing down on him. Ignoring the needle pricks in his bare arms and hands, he pulled himself the last few feet to safety and rolled on his side. From the corner of his eye he saw Nordea race back down the run ahead of the charging herd.

Lying there on the broken branches of the fallen spruce trees he watched as wave after wave of racing animals swept by. Eventually the herd thinned out until they were running in twos and threes and then they were gone.

He pushed to his knees, looked up the run, and his eyes found the two boys lying broken on the ground. He climbed down the tangle of limbs and dropped the last couple of feet, landing in a crouch on the forest floor. Taking a couple of steps in the direction of the boys, he was startled by a large buck that came running around the bend. The first thing he noticed was the wild frenzied look in its eyes, then he saw the two arrows, one sticking out of its front right shoulder and one in its hind quarter.

Seeing him directly in its path, the wounded caribou skidded to a halt. For a moment, they stared into each other's eyes. Then, as if recognizing that this was one of the kind that had inflicted the pain, the animal pawed the ground, lowered its heavily antlered head, and with a loud snort it charged.

Aboboneek slid the hathemay from his shoulder and reached back for an arrow. His searching fingers found nothing. The quiver was empty. They must have fallen out in his haste to climb the wall. He glanced toward the wall and saw one lying on the ground near the tangle of branches. It was a few steps away. Instinctively he knew there wasn't enough time get to it and get a shot off before the caribou would be on him, but he had to try. He turned and raced toward the arrow. Behind him he could hear the tortured breath of the wounded caribou as it came for him. He was almost there when he heard the deep throaty growl and saw the blur of black and white pass close to his side. He fell to the ground, grabbed the arrow, rolled to his knees and notched it in his hathemay in one fluid desperate motion. As he brought the hathemay up he saw Nordea launch herself at the charging animal's throat. It was enough to throw it off its path and it stumbled and slid by him, opening a small cut on his shoulder with an antler tip as it passed.

It struggled to get to its feet, violently shaking its head in a desperate attempt to dislodge its attacker. Nordea's fangs had found the artery and with each frantic beat of its heart, the lifeblood sprayed over the locked animals and dripped on the ground. It was quickly over. Aboboneek lowered his hathemay and slowly drew his knife. He held it at his side and waited. This was Nordea's first kill and he knew it would have awakened her wild instincts. She could be dangerous in the frenzy of the hunt. He stayed there on his knees and let her finish it.

When the caribou finally stopped moving Nordea released its neck from her jaws and backed away. She stood there for a moment licking the fresh blood from her muzzle, then turned and padded to Aboboneek's side. She settled back on her haunches and looked at him expectantly.

Aboboneek slipped the knife back into its sheath and reached over to scratch her ears. "Good girl," he said affectionately.

Her tail scattered the loose gravel as it swished the ground behind her.

Chapter 2
1719

Baroodisick was now sixteen. Aboboneek watched him affectionately as he walked ahead on the trail surrounded by a group of boys his own age. He carried himself well, Aboboneek noticed with pride. The others were intently listening to the story he was relating. He had that way about him; the ability to draw in his listeners with his colorful words and animated actions and make them feel as if they were living the story. He is a good boy, thought Aboboneek proudly.

The piece of red cloth decorating the tip of his hathemay fluttered in the wind above his head. The matching piece he had woven into the long braid swayed back and forth across his bare back as his head bobbed back and forth in the telling of the story. The upturned faces of his companions were evidence of the extent to which he had their attention.

Aboboneek smiled contentedly.

They were following the river trail on their way back to the coast. The winter had been spent inland and now that the snow had left the land, the tribe had begun the annual trek back to their summer camp.

Aboboneek and the boys were toward the back of the long caravan of thirty or more. Nordea padded along at his side. Shawwayet was toward the front of the procession with some of the other women and younger children.

She liked to travel with the younger children. It made her happy to be around them. They had only one other child, and she had died at birth. Now that Baroodisick was grown, she made it her mission to teach the younger ones all she knew about the history of the tribe. That's where he gets his storytelling skills from, thought Aboboneek.

A light breeze rustled the newly formed leaves in the trees along the path, giving a little relief from the bright sun that hung in the sky behind him. Sweat beaded on his neck and ran down his back underneath the heavy pack he carried on his shoulders. Just to the right of the path, the silver water of the rushing river raced ahead of him on its way to the sea. Swimming through its tides, the wasemook (salmon) occasionally broke through the surface in search of the insects that surfed the moving water.

This is a good place.

"Boom".

Everyone froze.

Baroodisick looked back at his father anxiously.

"Boom".

"What is it father?"

"I don't know, son. It's coming from farther downriver."

Suddenly, the orderly line that had gone silent in puzzled curiosity broke down into panicked disarray as the screams could be heard from the group at the front. Packs were dropped in the path as their frightened owners turned and ran.

Aboboneek stood to the side and watched them race by, watching for Shawwayet. He saw some of the smaller children being carried and others hustled down the path ahead of the hurrying adults, but he did not see Shawwayet. Everyone was crying and screaming.

With a sinking feeling, the realization that it must have been the gun of a Buggishaman (white man) he had heard began to wash over him. He had listened to the stories of their guns but he had never heard the sound before.

Where was Shawwayet, he wondered. She must have hidden in the woods.

He lifted the hathemay from his shoulder, notched an arrow, and slowly walked toward where the sound had come from. He placed his hand on the top of Nordea's head to caution her to be quiet. Four of his friends walked behind him with arrows at the ready.

It was quieter now. Most of the tribe had disappeared back down the path and into the woods. Just before the path bent around a turn in the river, he saw Baroodisick and the small group of boys standing there watching them. He motioned to them to keep going and then turned and led his group in the other direction.

He wondered what they would find. He had heard some of the cries of the women that had run by him. "They killed them," they had screamed as they raced into the woods. He hoped it wasn't true, but he feared it probably was.

The path bent to the left and cut across a wide clearing, a rippling sea of yellow flowers. Stepping from the woods into the clearing, Aboboneek came to a sudden halt. Spread before him was a scene that he knew would be burned into his memory until the day he died.

Close to them lay one of the older men of the tribe. His back was bloodied and torn, and he was not moving. Just a few steps beyond him lay the motionless body of one of the little girls, her face buried in the grass where she had fallen. His eyes continued along the trail and came to rest on Shawwayet. Her lifeless eyes were staring up at the sky. Her left arm was draped protectively around one of the toddlers she had been carrying. Aboboneek threw back his head and screamed in anguish. Nordea answered with her primal howl.

One of the two Buggishaman standing near the bodies raised his gun and fired. Aboboneek heard the thud and short cry of alarm as the man next to him took the full force of the shot. The four of them released their arrows and scrambled into the woods as another shot tore through the brush where they had been standing.

"I will not leave her."

"How can the four of us take them with their guns?"

"We will wait. They must sleep sometime."

"Perhaps they will leave."

"No. They have settled here. They have a tent at the edge of the woods."

"It will be dark soon."

"I will go and bring the rest of the men of the tribe."

"Take Baroodisick with you," said Aboboneek. "I don't want him here for this. Hurry back."

While he waited for the others to arrive, Aboboneek sat alone, at little distance from his friends. He sat with his back against the trunk of a tree with his head in his hands. He sobbed softly.

Nordea lay quietly by his side, watching him through her half-closed eyes.

What did Shawwayet do to deserve this? She would never hurt anyone. Why would they have shot her, and those little children? What kind of animal would do such a thing? They must pay for this. Why couldn't they leave us alone?

"I will kill them," he muttered softly. "They have no place here." Nordea lifted her head and watched him intently. Her ears quivered and twitched anxiously.

As the sun dipped behind the distant hills and night began to quietly cloak the land in darkness, Aboboneek could see the flicker of the Buggishaman's campfire through the trees. It was close to the river's edge, away from the surrounding woods.

That's a good thing, he thought. The noise of the river will cover our approach. They probably won't expect us to come back either.

Soon the others arrived, slipping quietly into the small space where they waited. They watched Aboboneek expectantly, waiting for him to speak. There were now ten of them.

Whispering quietly, Aboboneek began. "We will take the two Buggishaman first. After we kill them, we will gather the bodies of our tribe and take them back upriver."

In the pale light of the partial moon, he drew in the dirt with one of his arrows. He drew the river and the woods that outlined the clearing. Using small stones, he showed them where the Buggishaman's tent sat in the clearing and where the bodies of Shawwayet and the others lay.

Choosing three of the men, he pointed to the river. "We will approach the tent in the water. The rest of you will space yourselves around the edge of the clearing in the woods. When we are in position, we will signal and you will all scream the war cry. Their backs will be turned to us and we will rush them from the river."

Around the circle, the squatting men nodded in acknowledgement. Each in turn touched their forehead and then their chest over their hearts. Aboboneek returned each salute. They knew there was always a chance they would not all make it through this. Aboboneek was grateful they had all come to support him.

One of the men indicated Nordea. "What about her?"

"She will do as she pleases," replied Aboboneek. "If she howls it will add to their confusion."

"What will be the signal?"

"The whistle of the night bird; when you hear that it will be time to begin."

Aboboneek stood to his feet. He watched as the men quietly melted into the surrounding woods. Then he and the three who remained slipped off their clothes and waded into the river. Each of them grasped a knife in their teeth.

Slipping beneath the chilly water, they made their way downstream. Only their heads remained above the surface.

Aboboneek used the flicker of their fire to mark the Buggishaman's position as he led the procession. He moved far enough downriver to place the tent between him and the fire, and then slowly crawled through the shallow water with his comrades until they were all on the grass at the edge of the river.

They lay there on their bellies listening to the night sounds. The smell of the damp musty earth filled Aboboneek's nostrils. It was softly tainted with the smoke drifting over them from the dying fire.

He could almost reach out and touch the tent from where he lay. Inside, someone breathed the relaxed breath of sleep. He wondered if one or both were inside. It was more likely one of them was sitting by the fire, watching, he thought.

Touching the two men on his left, he motioned toward the tent. To the other one he waved his hand for him to follow as he slid through the grass on his belly toward the end of the tent. Just as he expected, he saw the other Buggishaman sitting next to the fire with his gun cradled in his lap, facing the woods.

Slowly, he pulled himself into the crouched position and watched his companion do the same. Turning back to the two at the tent he waited until the knife had sliced a hole in the canvas side.

Then he whistled.

The Buggishaman at the fire whirled around at the sound, bringing up the barrel of the gun as he turned. The night was split with the blood curdling screams in the surrounding woods, accompanied by the hair-raising howl of the moisamadrook. The Buggishaman hesitated and then turned back and fired into the trees. It was long enough for Aboboneek and his companion to cover the ground between them. Their knives found their targets and the struggle was quickly over.

Aboboneek glanced over his shoulder at the tent as the bloodied tribesmen emerged. He turned and began the long walk across the field to Shawwayet. Nordea sidled out from the woods and padded along beside him.

Chapter 3
1722

Baroodisick wondered why he hadn't noticed her before. She had been with the tribe as long as he had, longer in fact, she was a year older than him.

It was as if she had been invisible to him until just recently. Now everywhere he looked she was there. Perhaps that was because he seemed to be going out of his way to make sure he was in the same place as her. It was as if something had taken over and was persistently nudging him in her direction.

He had no idea what it was, but he liked it. Of course, he couldn't let the other guys see it. They wouldn't understand and would only give him a hard time.

"Dattomensh," he said softly. What a great name that was. He liked how it rolled off his tongue. "Dattomensh."

His eyes were drawn across the clearing, where a group of girls were painting themselves with odemet (red ochre). They were coating each other's bare backs where they couldn't easily reach themselves. Dattomensh was in animated conversation with the others. He heard her laughter. It stirred something deep in his chest. These feelings were new to him. Strange, but good.

She was the best-looking girl there. He watched as one of the girls rubbed the red dye into Dattomensh's back. He wished it were his hands.

He felt he was being watched and turned to see. His eyes met his father's. He was sitting on the ground in front of their mamateek with a wide grin across his face. Baroodisick dropped his eyes sheepishly.

Aboboneek chuckled softly. "When will you ask her, son?"

"Who? Ask her what?" Baroodisick stumbled over his words.

"You think I haven't noticed?"

Baroodisick did not respond.

"I've watched you follow her around."

Baroodisick moved to where his father was sitting and joined him on the ground. He still had a good view of the girls and found his eyes straying from time to time. The last time he looked up, he met Dattomensh's eyes across the clearing. She smiled at him and he totally missed what his father was saying.

"What?"

"I was saying she is a great girl. She comes from a strong family. She would make a good wife for you."

"You think so?" Baroodisick asked, not hiding the pleasure in his voice.

"Yes, I do," smiled Aboboneek. "I think you should ask her."

The wedding celebrations took place in the middle of the summer. The sun had been shining its warmth in abundance all week long; one of those rare times on the island when the wind didn't blow.

There must have been 200 people gathered for the celebration. Word had gotten out and people had been filtering in for the last couple of weeks. Weddings were an opportunity to visit with family and old friends and everyone was taking advantage of it.

Hunters had brought in several caribou, rabbits, and other small animals. Eggs had been gathered from the bird islands and baskets of wasemook were being cleaned for the feast that would take place tomorrow.

Baroodisick and Dattomensh sat on the ground next to his father's mamateek watching the activity. There were people everywhere. The clearing was filled with laughter. Children were chasing each other, yelling and squealing with delight. It was a noisy and happy place.

Baroodisick slipped his hand in hers. "This is all for you," he said softly.

Dattomensh smiled and rested her head on his shoulder. Her long black hair fell across his bare chest. He gently kissed the top of her head and buried his face in her hair, filling his nostrils with the familiar oily scent he had come to know so well.

Overhead, the large, round silver moon watched them as they held each other tight before parting for the night, knowing tomorrow they would begin their journey as husband and wife.

The day started early. The cooking fires were stoked and the meat pots were full. In the centre of the field, a place had been cleared for the games, which had already gotten underway when Baroodisick emerged from his father's mamateek.

Targets were set up and the men and older boys were competing with arrows and axes. Younger children were playing their own games, tossing stones and short sticks. A thick rope that must have been taken from a settler had been tied to the branch of a tree and was being used as a swing by some of the older girls. The clearing was abuzz with shouts of laughter and good-natured ribbing.

Baroodisick looked around him at all the familiar faces. This was a happy day; for him, the happiest. This day he would be married to Dattomensh.

One of the women walked by him carrying a bowl of steaming wasemook, heading for the large square house that had been built to hold the ceremony and feast. Smiling broadly, she said, "This is your day, Baroodisick."

Turning, he stepped back into the mamateek. It was time to get ready. The drums would sound before long, summoning everyone to the ceremony.

Using the water that had been warming by the fire, he washed his long hair, re-braided it carefully, and applied a liberal coating of oil. A thin beam of sunlight filtered through the smoke hole in the roof, striking his long braid so it shone in the light. At the end of the braid he tied a new piece of red cloth. He put aside a matching piece to replace the old worn one at the tip of his hathemay. Next, he applied a fresh coat of odemet to his entire body, thinking as he did that Dattomensh was doing the same in her mamateek. He smiled as the picture flashed through his mind.

When he finished applying the odemet, he slipped on the newly fringed cloak his father was holding.

"You look good, my son," said Aboboneek affectionately, wrapping him in a bear hug. "I wish your mother could have been here to see you today."

Baroodisick looked into the moist eyes of his father and replied. "I'm sure she is watching, father."

Outside, the drum began its slow rhythmic beat.

Aboboneek and Baroodisick sat on the ground next to the fire to wait for the beat to change, signalling that everyone was inside and it was time for the bride and groom to enter.

They sat quietly, each lost in their own thoughts, comfortable in the prolonged silence.

The everyday chatter and noises began to dwindle in the clearing outside and soon the beat changed. The two of them pushed to their feet and walked out of the mamateek into the deserted clearing.

Side by side, they walked across the beaten ground to the entrance to the large community mamateek. As they stepped inside, the drummer changed the beat once again and everyone fell silent and found a place on the floor.

Baroodisick's eyes were drawn to the entrance in the opposite end of the mamateek. Silhouetted in the doorway stood Dattomensh, flanked by her mother and father. She had never looked so beautiful. His face broke into a wide smile as their eyes met.

Once more the drummer changed to a slow beat and they began the long walk toward each other. They all met in the centre of the house and turned to face the chief who was standing there holding the ceremonial arrow.

He was an impressive figure with his long braid filled with colorful feathers and his bare chest painted with symbols signifying his status as chief.

He raised his hands, commanding silence, and smiled at his niece as she stood before him.

To the those who had gathered, he said, "Behold these two who have come before me today to marry. Bear witness to their desire to be united. Accept this new family into yours and treat them as your own."

To the party standing before him, he asked, "Who brings this girl to be married?"

"We do," said Dattomensh's father.

"Who brings this boy to be married?"

"I do," said Aboboneek proudly.

Chief Tatamunchaa waited for the three parents to find a seat and then continued. "Today you have all witnessed the presentation of these two, Dattomensh and Baroodisick, by their parents. By your presence, you tell them that you as a tribe member will support them and honour them as a family."

"Kneel before me children," he said to the bride and groom.

Obediently they followed his instruction. Baroodisick reached out and curled his hand around Dattomensh's and squeezed softly.

Tatamunchaa held the ceremonial arrow in both hands above their bowed heads. He snapped it in half and handed the tail to Dattomensh and the head to Baroodisick. "This symbolizes your union," he said. "The arrow must have a head and a tail to be complete, so must a marriage have a bride and a groom. Together you are stronger. Together you become one. As chief, I declare you, Dattomensh and Baroodisick, to be husband and wife. Rise as man and woman and begin your journey together."

Baroodisick took Dattomensh by the hand and lifted her to her feet. He reached into the small bag tied to his waist and removed the necklace he'd been working on over the past few weeks. The pieces of shiny tin he had shaped and shined for hours were interspersed with colored beads from the Buggishaman. His heart leaped as he saw the delight in Dattomensh's eyes when she saw the necklace. She bowed her head to allow him to slip it on and then reached up and kissed him on the lips.

The mamateek erupted in celebration.

Chapter 4
1723

Aboboneek watched as Nordea limped across the clearing. She had lived beyond her years just as he had. In all that time, she had not returned to the wild but had stayed by his side. He reached out and affectionately scratched her ears as she stretched out on the ground next to him. She leaned into his hand, relishing the contact. Aboboneek smiled contentedly.

He knew she sensed he was not well. She had stayed closer to him lately, mostly hunting when he slept.

Things had changed for him a few days after Baroodisick's wedding. Without warning, he had begun to experience excruciating pains in his head that left him with blurred sight and slurred speech, sometimes lasting for days. It left him confused and disorientated. Although it eventually wore off after each episode, it did not leave him the same. It was as if a piece of him was taken away each time. Memories were taken from him as well. Sometimes he couldn't remember what had happened earlier that same day, yet scenes from his youth were crystal clear. Soon there would be nothing left, he feared.

The first episode had happened without warning. Baroodisick and Dattomensh had left the morning after the wedding for a two-week trip upriver to the Great Lake. Aboboneek left camp around the same time to do some hunting. He and Nordea had headed in the opposite direction, following the river toward the coast.

About an hour into his trip, without any warning, the wave of pain washed over him, turning his vision black and dropping him to his knees. Someone from the tribe had eventually found him there and brought him home.

When Baroodisick returned, his father was back on his feet, seemingly no worse for wear. However, it did not last long.

The episodes were happening more frequently, and seemed to last longer. He knew he did not have long. One of them would take him soon, he was sure of that. He hoped it did not happen until after Dattomensh's baby arrived. That would be any day now, maybe today.

Running his hand down Nordea's side as she lay stretched out on the ground with her back nestled up to his leg, he spoke softly to her. "It's our time, girl. We will soon begin a new journey to Gossett (land of the dead). I will cross the river alone. You must stay and watch over my family."

Nordea lifted her head and stared into his eyes. Understanding seemed to pass between them and she laid her head back on the ground as he continued scratching her side.

Behind him he heard the door of the mamateek being pushed aside and Baroodisick rushed past them. "The baby is coming," he said breathlessly. "I have to get help."

A few moments later he returned with the old woman who delivered all the babies of the camp. They brushed past Aboboneek and Nordea and entered the mamateek.

Aboboneek listened to the noises inside for a while and then he leaned his head back against the mamateek and closed his eyes.

Baroodisick found him slumped to the side when he brought the baby out for him to see. He knew he was gone and would not return this time. The spirits had exchanged one life for the other. He gazed into his son's eyes with a mixture of sadness and joy. Nordea watched him as she protectively rested her head on Aboboneek's legs.

"You shall be called Haddowaddet," he said softly. "You will always carry my father's spirit." A stray tear splashed on his son's upturned face.

They buried Aboboneek the next day on a small hill overlooking the river. Nordea did not return to the camp with them. She lay on the fresh mound of dirt and no amount of coaxing would entice her to leave.

Two days later, Baroodisick returned to visit the grave and she was gone.

Chapter 5
1730

Haddowaddet and his mother were travelling to the coast to trade with the Buggishaman. For the last two years, this had become a regular occurrence for the tribe but this was the first time for Haddowaddet. His mother carried several animal skins in the pack slung over her shoulder. She hoped to trade for clothes, beads, and other shiny objects the Buggishaman might have.

They were travelling with another twenty or so women and children from the tribe and it was a noisy and happy procession. The men seldom accompanied them on these trips. They hunted the furs and the women traded them. That was just the way it was.

Haddowaddet ran and shouted with several other boys as they made their way along the coast to where the Buggishaman had set up the trading camp.

There were lots of things to see and explore along the coast, and Haddowaddet was determined not to miss a thing. Yesterday was the first time he saw the ocean. The other boys had told him about it but nothing had prepared him for how big it was. It went on forever. When they had walked out of the woods and it lay there in front of him he had been spellbound. He stopped in his tracks and just stared. A tiny island with a bunch of stunted trees sat in the water a little way off from shore but beyond that there was nothing to see but water.

"Look mother," he said when he finally found his voice. "It's so big."

Dattomensh smiled at his wonder.

"Where does it come from? Can I touch it?"

Dattomensh dropped her bag, grabbed his hand, and they ran down the beach together. At the water's edge, she stopped and let go of his hand. The water ran up the sand, washed over his feet, and retreated again. He wriggled his toes, laughed with delight, and stepped out farther.

He stood there letting the waves wash around him, splashing over the tips of his fingers. Lifting his hand to his mouth, he tasted the water with his tongue and spat out the salty water with disgust. He glanced back at his mother questioningly.

"You can't drink that water, Haddowaddet," she said laughing at the expression on his face.

He wiped his arm across his mouth to remove what remained of the bitter water and turned back. He watched the waves around his feet for a while and then reached down and picked up a shell that had tumbled along next to his foot, and then another. Soon he had too many to carry in his hands and he began to throw them up on the sand where his mother was sitting.

"Come here, Haddowaddet," she called. "We have enough now."

Reluctantly he waded ashore and joined her on the beach. "We have to keep those," he said. "We can make a necklace for you, mother."

"They're pretty, Haddowaddet. Let's sort them and pick the best ones. They will make a beautiful necklace."

Haddowaddet was watching some of his friends farther down the beach where it ended in a tall cliff. They seemed to have found a small cave. Some of the bigger waves were smashing into the water side of the cliff, sending a cloud of white spray over the group.

Dattomensh saw where he was looking. "Go ahead," she said. "But stay out of the water over there. It will carry you away."

He jumped to his feet and raced off in their direction.

She sat in the sand and watched him run, thinking back to when he was born, smiling at his excitement. Life is good, she thought as she leaned back on her arms and turned her face up to the warm sun.

On the second day, they followed the coastline until the sun reached the middle of the sky and then had lunch on the grass near the beach. Once lunch was finished, Dattomensh stuffed the remaining food into her bag and called Haddowaddet back from the beach where he was examining the small rounded stones. He selected two, dropped the rest, and ran back to where his mother stood. Then they left the beach and struck out across country, following the trail of those ahead. The trail would lead them through the woods to the coast on the other side.

It was later in the afternoon when those in the lead walked out of the woods and spotted the camp across a large barren open space that led down to the water's edge. The Buggishaman had set up several cloth tents with colored ribbons tied to the centre posts. As they all bunched up at the edge of the woods, one of the women pointed at the strips of colored cloth fluttering in the windy breeze and exclaimed excitedly. "Look at that!" The whole group began to hurry across the clearing, no longer walking in single file but spread out across the field. Each of the women intent on finding the treasures of the Buggishaman before the other.

Several Buggishaman emerged from the tents and watched the group approach. Haddowaddet could hear them laughing and shouting to each other in their strange language. It was all very exciting. He was glad his mother had let him come on this trip. He was having so much fun.

When the group reached the tents, they split up and the bartering began in earnest.

Haddowaddet followed his mother, who headed for the tent at the end where there were several colored blankets spread on the ground. One of the blankets was covered with colored beads and small pieces of rounded glass with bright colors running through the inside of them. Another blanket was covered with small shiny pots and containers. The third had stacks of blankets and pieces of cloth. Dattomensh knelt on the blanket with the beads and began to examine the trinkets. The Buggishaman hovered nearby. Haddowaddet stayed standing and watched him warily. He had never been this close to one of them before. It made him nervous and he stayed near the edge of the blanket where his mother was kneeling.

The Buggishaman wore loose, baggy pants stuffed into boots that reached almost to his knees. His multicolored shirt was open almost to the waist revealing a broad chest covered in thick black hair. At his side, he carried a short gun in a leather sling. His shoulder-length hair was tied in a pigtail at the back and his coal black beard was trimmed close to his face. His eyes were what troubled Haddowaddet the most. They were the color of the sky and they seemed to pierce through him whenever their eyes met, forcing him to quickly look away.

Dattomensh selected one of the blankets and a handful of the colored trinkets. She pulled a fox skin from the pack she carried and held it out to the Buggishaman. He took it and inspected it closely, turning it inside out and sniffing it carefully. Satisfied, he nodded his head and held out his hand for more. Dattomensh shook her head, no. He wagged the hand he had extended toward her and said, "Not enough." Dattomensh clutched her bag against her chest and shook her head no, again.

Haddowaddet began to get uneasy as he watched the Buggishaman's face grow dark with anger.

"Let's go," said Dattomensh to Haddowaddet. "That is all he is going to get for this."

"Are you sure, mother? He looks dangerous. Give him the other skin," he said nervously.

"No. We need that to trade with the others."

Dattomensh turned her back and walked away.

"Come back here." yelled the Buggishaman. Haddowaddet didn't understand the words but he understood the tone, and he was suddenly very scared. He wished his mother would give the Buggishaman the other fur.

Everyone stopped what they were doing and turned to see what the commotion was.

Dattomensh kept going.

Haddowaddet, who was hurrying to catch her, looked over his shoulder at the Buggishaman in time to see him pull the gun from its sling. The little puff of smoke and the loud bang made him jump. He turned to his mother only to find her face down on the ground. Blood was spreading through her cloak where the shot had torn through her back. She was not moving. Colored beads lay on the ground where they had scattered from her hand.

For a moment, everyone stood frozen, and then, as if on signal, the whole group of tribe members dropped everything and ran for the woods.

Haddowaddet backed away from the Buggishaman who now had the gun pointed at him. A slight smile pulled up the corners of his mouth underneath those piercing blue eyes. Haddowaddet shivered in fear. The Buggishaman matched him, step for step until he reached Dattomensh.

Torn between his need to help his mother and the fear of the Buggishaman, Haddowaddet stopped backing away and stood there trembling in indecision. He watched as the Buggishaman picked up the beads, roughly rolled his mother on her back, and pulled the blanket from her bag along with the extra fur. He dumped the rest of the contents on the ground, scattered them with his fingers, and seeing nothing that interested him, left them there.

He pushed to his feet and stared at Haddowaddet standing there alone, in the middle of the meadow. With a loud roar, he lunged in the direction of the boy, raised the pistol in the air, and fired.

Haddowaddet whirled around and bolted for the safety of the woods.

Chapter 6
1740

Haddowaddet and his father had moved away from the coast shortly after Dattomensh was killed. They had joined a band who had settled about a day's journey inland on the Great River. Ten years had passed since then.

Haddowaddet stilled remembered the events of that terrible day, but the bad dreams had finally ceased.

Life was quieter here, away from the Buggishaman, and except for the occasional excursion to the coast, the band had no contact with them. It was just as well because Haddowaddet hated them so much he wanted nothing more than to kill them like they had killed his mother. He longed to find the Buggishaman with the blue eyes again. He would love to kill him. It was all he deserved.

His father had eventually talked him out of launching his own personal war on them, arguing the pointlessness of his plan, but he knew someday he would find a way to avenge his mother's murder. There was little doubt in his mind why his father had moved him out of the coastal area so quickly. He'd had no intention of risking losing his son.

The years had done little to lessen the ill-will he felt toward the Buggishaman, but lately his mind had been filled with other, more pressing matters.

The most beautiful girl he had ever seen had just recently moved into the camp.

Returning from a hunting trip two days ago, he had been following the path when he'd heard someone singing down by the river. The sound of her voice made him stop. He'd stood there on the trail, listened for a moment, and then impulsively decided to check it out.

Leaving the trail, he quietly pushed through the thick bushes until he reached the river's edge. He did not want to make a noise and risk interrupting the singing, so he moved carefully, watching where he stepped. Here at the river's edge, the singing that had drawn him was clearer. He had heard singing before, in fact lots of it. It was always a part of the ceremonies, but that was different. Most of the time it was loud, fast-talking, to the beat of a drum and the thump of dancing feet. This voice had no accompaniment, nor did it need any. There was a soothing sound to it; the way the words were strung together, sometimes marching, sometimes lightly stepping; the way her voice rose and fell. It was as if he could feel the song deep inside of him.

He'd looked downriver and saw her for the first time.

She was sitting at the water's edge with her feet immersed in the gently flowing river, leaning back on her two arms with her hands firmly planted on the ground behind her. Her upturned face was soaking in the warm sun, her long shiny hair splayed over the grass between her hands. Her eyes were tightly closed and she was singing as if she were the only one in the world.

Haddowaddet was spellbound. He hadn't remembered feeling wonder like this since the day he had first seen the ocean. After a few moments had passed, he realized he was holding his breath and let it out with an audible whoosh, breaking the spell.

She opened her eyes, slowly turned her head, and looked at him curiously.

"Where did you come from?" she asked.

Her voice sounded as good to him when she spoke as it did when she was singing. "Nowhere," he mumbled, suddenly feeling very self-conscious.

"Nowhere is not a place," she said.

"I meant…." he began.

"You can't be from Nowhere," she interrupted. "You have to be from Somewhere."

"I am."

"Are you?"

"Yes."

She watched him with her head slightly tilted to the side. Her eyes twinkled with amusement. She swirled her bare feet in the water, creating ripples that spread and quickly disappeared downstream in the flowing river.

He took a deep breath. She was confusing him, and why was his heart beating so fast, he wondered. A nervous tension had gripped his body and was doing strange things inside his chest. His tongue seemed to have gotten thicker and he wasn't sure he would be able to speak properly, even if he had the slightest idea what to say to this girl.

Luckily, she finally broke the silence.

"You're from the camp, aren't you? I've seen you there."

"Yes," he mumbled, relieved that the word came out right, "I am."

"You live in the mamateek at the edge of the clearing between the three tall birch trees."

He nodded, wondering how she would have noticed that. There were about twelve mamateeks in the clearing. Why would she have paid any attention to his?

"Hunting, were you?" she nodded to the two rabbits hanging from his belt.

"I like your singing," he blurted out.

She smiled and his mind went blank again.

"Come and sit," she said, patting the grass next to her.

He fumbled with the string holding the rabbits. Finally, he got them untied, dropped them on the ground, and slipped his hathemay from his shoulder, placing it, along with his arrows, next to them. Then he walked to her side and sat on the grass next to her.

His heart was racing again and his throat was uncomfortably dry. Sitting so close to this beautiful creature was both frightening and exciting at the same time. It was a little like the final moments of the hunt, just before releasing the arrow.

As he placed his hand on the grass to support himself, his fingers touched hers and a flash of current coursed through him so strong that he looked down to see if there were actual sparks there.

She began talking again.

He concentrated on keeping his fingers next to hers.

"What's your name?"

"What?"

"Your name. What's your name?"

"Haddowaddet."

"Have you always lived at the camp?"

"No, we lived far from here, close to the sea. My father and I moved here when I was seven. That was ten years ago." He realized he was talking just fine, despite the strange sensations coursing through him. Somehow, he realized, she was making it easy for him to talk.

"Where is your mother?"

"She was murdered by the Buggishaman," he spat out a little too forcefully.

"I'm sorry."

Immediately regretting speaking as he did, he said, "That is why we left the coast. Father wanted to make sure we had no further contact with the Buggishaman."

"You sound angry, Haddowaddet."

"I am. I will avenge her someday."

"Anger will take all your happiness, Haddowaddet," she said softly. "It will leave no room for joy."

"But I owe it to my mother."

"Perhaps you do, but maybe she wouldn't want that for you."

Haddowaddet stared into her eyes. In those shimmering dark pools, he saw a kindness and warmth he had not felt since his mother died. Somehow, they seemed to reach into him and fill some of the emptiness that had been left when he lost her that terrible day.

She met his gaze and did not turn away, finally reaching up to kiss him tenderly on the cheek.

"You haven't told me your name," he said.

"It's Gaboweete," she murmured.

"That means breath. How appropriate for you."

"What do you mean?" she said, idly splashing the water with her feet.

"You sing so beautifully."

"You think so?"

"Yes, I do. I have never heard such beautiful singing."

She dropped her eyes as she watched her toes wiggle in the shallow water.

"How come I haven't seen you at the camp?" he asked.

"We just arrived last week. We are on the way to the coast."

"Where is your Somewhere?"

"I grew up at the Great Lake," she laughed.

Her laugh made him smile. He wanted to hear more of it.

Chapter 7
1740

Three days later, Haddowaddet and Baroodisick left for a hunting trip into the interior. They had decided to hunt from an old camp about two day's journey, inland. For once, Haddowaddet wasn't excited about leaving the camp. Leaving camp meant leaving Gaboweete. He seemed to have developed an overpowering need to be near her. Problem was, he and his father had been planning this trip for more than a week and there was no way for him to get out of it. He'd even thought of feigning sickness, but he knew his father would probably see right through it. He consoled himself with the knowledge that they would only be gone a few days.

They left home in a light summer shower, the kind that seems to cleanse the air, leaving behind a fresh smell of watered plants and ripening berries. The soft wind was coaxing the moisture laden leaves to shake off their excess water, which fell to the forest floor and soaked into the thirsty roots that snaked through the ground below. Overhead, the noon day sun broke through the scattered clouds and soon had dried their damp clothes.

Haddowaddet noticed none of this. He was lost in thoughts of Gaboweete. Before this week, he had been looking forward to this trip, but since the chance meeting on the banks of the river, it no longer held the excitement for him that it did before. He would have rather stayed in camp where she was. She was all that filled his mind these past few days. He found himself in areas of the camp he never frequented before; places where the women worked that he would have avoided in the past. He knew the other boys were talking about him but he didn't care. Being near Gaboweete was all that mattered.

He wondered how she felt about him. Good, he thought. But this was all new to him and maybe the way she looked at him was the way she looked at all the boys. He didn't think so, but he wasn't sure. Then again, none of the other girls at the camp made him feel this way when they looked at him. Something was different. That he knew for sure.

The way she teased him made him feel good. It meant she noticed him, not the other boys, him.

He absentmindedly watched his father's back as he followed a few steps behind him. There was little of his surroundings that registered with him. He stepped around the large rocks in the trail without even seeing them. His thoughts were back at camp. Even though they had only just left, all he could think about was returning from the trip and seeing her again.

Most of the day had passed and he had no idea where it had gone. The sun was sinking behind the trees ahead of them when his father stopped in the path and announced they had gone as far as they would be going for the day. He looked at his son and said, "Where have you been all day? You realize you have barely said a word since we left camp?"

"Just been thinking, that's all."

"About Gaboweete, I suppose?"

"Mostly."

"Well its time to set up camp. See if you can get a fire going. I'll cut some branches and make a place to sleep."

Sometime later, as the evening shadows deepened, after they had eaten and were sitting around the fire, Haddowaddet asked his father, "Do you like her?"

"I don't know much about her, son. Her family has only been at camp a little while."

Haddowaddet sat in silence with his head bowed, staring into the flickering flames. He idly poked at the hot embers with a long stick.

Finally, he said, "I can't get her out of my mind, father."

Baroodisick, who was lying on the ground propped up on one elbow, watched his son. He understood the thoughts and feelings that were filling his son's head. He had been young once.

His mind drifted back to the time he had first seen Dattomensh. Like his son, he had been stricken and nothing else held any importance. Being near her was all that mattered. Young love was what stuck a relationship together, preparing it for the harder times that would eventually come as the years went by.

"She seems to live in my head. It's as if I can't think straight anymore."

"I know son. I felt that way about your mother. The next few weeks will be the best of your life. Hold onto them and enjoy them as much as you can."

The next day, they left the river they had been following and headed inland, deep into the interior where there were few signs that man had been there before. It was a beautiful country, teeming with life. The further they travelled through the thick woods and across wet grassy bogs the more wildlife they encountered.

Haddowaddet was enjoying himself. He had not been this far into the interior of the country before. For the first time in a long time, his mind was clear. He even forgot Gaboweete for a while.

Where he had been oblivious of his surroundings, he now saw the animals and birds in the forest around them. The chorus of songbirds that fluttered overhead in the higher branches and the rabbits and other small animals that scurried through the underbrush, unafraid of their passing, made the day pass quickly and served to brighten his mood.

The sun was directly overhead when they stopped for a rest at the head of a small pond. The water had been dammed by a family of beavers and only trickled out in a small stream. Haddowaddet watched one of them as he dragged a small tree through the water in the direction of the house it had built, just out from the other shore of the pond. Only the roof, a tangle of interwoven sticks, was visible above the water, and when the beaver reached it, he slipped beneath the surface, taking the tree with him.

While he had been watching this, his father had started a fire and was roasting the partridge he had shot earlier. Haddowaddet sat on the ground next to the fire. He took the piece of partridge his father was holding out to him and bit into the hot meat.

"How much farther, Father?" he asked as he juggled the hot meat inside his mouth.

"We are almost there. We will be at the old camp before dark."

"When were you there last?"

"It's been years. May not be anything left of the mamateeks, unless someone else repaired them."

"How many?"

"Two."

"Have the Buggishaman ever been there?"

"No. They mostly stay at the coast or near the rivers. They have never ventured this far inland. They have not spoiled this part of the country. At least not yet."

"That is good."

"Yes son, that is good. They are slowly taking over the coast. The day will come when it will no longer be safe to go there."

"Why do they think they can take what they want?"

"I don't know Haddowaddet. It seems they don't consider us important. We are just a nuisance to them. Sometimes I don't think they believe we are people."

"Do you think they all think that way?"

"Probably not. I'm sure there are some who are good people. After all, they have families and children just like us. Problem is there is no way to tell which ones are good and which are bad. It's safer to believe they are all bad."

"I will never forgive them for killing mother."

"I know."

Just as his father had said, they reached the camp just as the sun slipped behind the hills in the distance, coloring the edge of the sky a golden red. They had crested a small hill and what remained of the camp was spread across the overgrown clearing in the valley below them. The mamateeks were stripped bare of their coverings and only the framing poles, some still standing but most lying haphazardly on the ground, marked where they had once been. The remnants of a tapaithook lay on the ground near the edge of the lake, little more than a frame left.

The clearing, which once had been trampled down and worn smooth, was now covered in tall ragged grass and young sprouting trees. It was easy to see no one had passed that way in a long time.

"We've got some work to do." muttered Baroodisick. "But that is for tomorrow. Let's find a place to sleep.

Early the next morning they began work on one of the mamateeks. First, they sorted out the fallen poles and restacked them to form the frame. Then they cut and stripped large sheets of rind from birch trees in the surrounding woods and spread them on the newly built frame, placing more poles around the outside to keep the birch rind in place. Lastly, they scooped mud from the edge of the lake and packed it around the seams to keep the wind out.

By the time it was finished, the sun was setting over the lake and another day had passed. The quiet chirping of evening song birds was the only sound, save for the lonely call of a loon somewhere out on the lake.

"The only thing we are missing is a covering for the door," said Baroodisick. "We will find a caribou or washawet tomorrow and take care of that."

Bone weary, Haddowaddet walked inside, lay on the ground, and was soon fast asleep.

Baroodisick sat on the ground next to him, watching him sleep and listening to the comforting night sounds outside. It reminded him of hunting trips with his father. It was good to get away like this with Haddowaddet. There might not be many more of these trips. He expected Haddowaddet would soon be married and then would come the children. Trips like this would be harder then. He was surprised he had managed to pull this one off, the way Haddowaddet had been smitten with Gaboweete.

I wonder how many children they will have, he thought. I think it will be fun to be a grandpa. I hope the first one is a boy. There is so much I can teach him, so many stories I must tell him.

Baroodisick smiled in the darkness.

The next morning, they slipped their hathemays on their shoulders and set out to explore the area around the lake in search of the best hunting spots. They hoped to bag several smaller animals like fox and rabbit to get their furs for trade at the coast, but they also needed a larger skin for the mamateek door, and food for the week at the camp.

Haddowaddet was excited, a little nervous at hunting something bigger like a washawet, but excited to be hunting with his father. He had tagged along with some of the larger hunting parties before but this was different. There were only the two of them, alone out here in the wilderness. They had this place all to themselves. Just them and the animals.

They followed the outline of the lake for a while, watching for animal signs. As they walked, his father pointed out tracks he had not spotted and told him what animal they belonged to. He showed him the fresh young shoots that had been bitten through by rabbits as they ran. They found a den where a fox had made a home. They decided they would return for that one later.

Soon they struck out across a large bog in search of caribou, keeping to the edge of the woods as they travelled.

At the far end, the water drained into a small brook which they followed into a clearing.

Suddenly Baroodisick stopped and held up his hand. "Listen," he whispered. Haddowaddet had heard it too and turned just as the caribou came crashing through the underbrush into the clearing. Baroodisick had already notched an arrow and released it as the animal came to a halt in front of them. His second arrow and Haddowaddet's first brought it down. Baroodisick ran to it and dispensed it with his knife.

Haddowaddet was walking toward them when he saw movement out of the corner of his eye. Two Indian men had entered the clearing. They were not Beothuk. He could tell by the color of their skin. They wore only loin cloths and a bunch of feathers in their hair. Their skin was not painted red, but they both had markings on their chests and arms. The younger one had an arrow notched in his hathemay. They were breathing heavily as if they had been running.

"Father." said Haddowaddet in warning.

Hearing the alarm in his son's voice, Baroodisick turned and saw the two Indians. Slowly he stood to his feet with the bloody knife held in his hand.

He knew what had happened here. He had noticed the other arrow sticking out of the caribou's throat. Now they were here to claim their animal. These were Micmac. They were friends of the settlers, not the Beothuk.

They might have put their arrow in the caribou first but his arrows had brought it down. He stood protectively over the animal.

The older Micmac began to shout, gesturing at the dead caribou. It was clear he was asserting his ownership.

"I think he is saying it is his," said Haddowaddet.

"I know. We killed the animal. It's ours."

"Are you going to fight them for it?" asked Haddowaddet nervously.

"If that is what it takes."

Clutching his father's hathemay in one hand and his own in the other, Haddowaddet began to move toward his father. The only other movement was the fluttering red ribbon tied to the tip of Baroodisick's hathemay.

The older Micmac shouted again and raised his hathemay. Haddowaddet stopped.

He motioned with his hathemay for Baroodisick to move away from the caribou.

Baroodisick shook his head no and raised the knife to the level of his waist.

The younger Micmac released his arrow, embedding it deep in Baroodisick's thigh.

The knife slipped from his hand as he grabbed at the arrow sticking out of his leg. He gave a low moan of pain when his hand touched the shaft and he fell backward to the ground.

Haddowaddet dropped the two hathemay and backed away from the Indians until he reached his father. Both had arrows notched and were pointing them at him.

When he reached his father's side, he bent and helped him to his feet. The arrow had passed through and he could see the arrowhead on the other side of the leg.

They turned their backs on the Indians and, leaning heavily on his son, Baroodisick limped out of the clearing without looking back.

Following the brook, Haddowaddet supported his father until they reached the edge of the bog. There they both collapsed in the long grass.

"We've got to get this out," said Baroodisick, grimacing in pain.

"How?"

"You have to break off the tail of the arrow close to my leg and pull it through."

"Me?"

"Yes. I can't do it myself."

"That shaft is as thick as my finger. I can't break that off."

"Use your knife and notch it out. Try not to move it much. But, cut a piece of branch from that tree first. I need something to bite down on."

Haddowaddet pulled his knife from its sheath, cut the branch, and gave it to his father. Then he tentatively placed the blade on the shaft of the arrow. Baroodisick groaned with pain.

Haddowaddet hesitated and looked at his father.

"Go ahead son. It has to be done," said Baroodisick through clenched teeth.

Slowly and carefully, he sliced into the arrow's shaft, cutting as close to his father's bleeding thigh as he dared. Each time the shaft moved, his father groaned in pain. He moved the knife around the shaft to make each cut until the two pieces were connected by a thin point at the centre. Holding the shaft on each side of the cut, he applied pressure and the arrow snapped.

"That was the easy part," gasped his father. "Now you have to pull it through."

He wiped the beads of sweat from his forehead and placed the piece of branch back between his teeth.

"Do it fast," he mumbled.

Haddowaddet grasped the arrowhead with his right hand but quickly let go, feeling something sticky. He looked down to find the palm of his hand covered in a wet black substance, mixed with his father's blood.

"What's this?"

"What?"

He held out his hand to show his father.

Baroodisick touched it with the tip of his finger and held it to his nose.

"They coated it with something to bring the caribou down," he said in alarm.

Haddowaddet looked into his father's eyes and saw a momentary flash of fear before he looked away.

"Go ahead and pull it out."

Baroodisick leaned back against the trunk of the tree and bit down on the branch. He closed his eyes and nodded.

Haddowaddet gripped the end of the arrow with one hand and placed the other against his father's leg, next to the bloody shaft. He took a deep breath and yanked. The shaft came free with a sucking noise followed by a gush of watery black blood.

His father was now slumped over on the ground, having passed out from the pain.

Haddowaddet wrapped the red ribbon he had removed from his father's braid around the bleeding leg and tied it as tight as he could. Then, he sat back on the ground and waited for his father to wake.

Overhead, the startled song birds had returned and were cheerily calling to one another in the branches of the trees. A soft breeze rustled the leaves, providing some relief from the hot noonday sun. They were at least an hour from the lake and had to cross the bog to get there. That wasn't going to be easy with his father's injured leg. Haddowaddet was scared; he was not sure he could do this. They were out here alone. There was no one to help them, and then there were the two Indians to worry about. But again, if the Indians wanted to kill them they would not have let them leave. They just wanted their caribou.

His father's fingers twitched and his eyes popped open as he released his breath like a gust of wind. His hand instinctively went to the wrap on his leg and he stiffened with pain. His eyes finally focused and he saw his son watching him anxiously.

With a sheepish grin he said, "Well I hope I don't ever have to do that again."

Haddowaddet gave him a tentative smile, but inside he was thinking about that black paste. If the Indians had coated the arrow head to help bring down the caribou, what was it going to do to his father? They needed to get to the lake to wash out the wound. Even then they might not get the poison out. He was worried.

"Can you walk, father?"

"Sure," replied Baroodisick with a confidence he didn't feel. "Probably should cut a stick for me to lean on."

Haddowaddet returned a few minutes later with a long pole he had cut from the trunk of a small tree. He had removed all the limbs, leaving one at the top that formed a v shape for his father to tuck under his arm for support. He helped him stand to his feet, wrapped his free arm around his neck for support, and they began the long walk back to the lake.

Progress was painfully slow with many rest stops along the way. The gash had stiffened up and the bandage was soaked in blood. With each step, Baroodisick groaned in pain. Each time they stopped he thought he would not get up again, but Haddowaddet kept pushing him. What had taken them no more than an hour in the morning, took them half the day now. It was getting dark when they reached the edge of the lake.

They collapsed in exhaustion on the grass at the water's edge. Haddowaddet untied the bandage, scooped water from the lake, and washed the mess from his father's leg that was now red and swollen. He sliced a piece from the bottom of his cloak and wrapped it again. Then he leaned back on the ground next to his father and they fell asleep where they lay.

Haddowaddet was awaken by his father's shouts. Much of what he was saying he couldn't understand. He was flailing around in his sleep, swinging his arms wildly over his head. In the pale light of the early morning he could see the bandage was soaked and the leg had swollen even more overnight.

With alarm, he leaned over his father and grabbed his swinging arms.

"Father, father," he shouted in his face.

His father's unseeing eyes opened. He yanked his arm free and swung at Haddowaddet, landing a glancing blow on the side of his head, knocking him back on the ground.

Haddowaddet shook his head in surprise and scooted out of reach.

Baroodisick's arms went limp and fell to the ground at his side. He was silent and still.

Haddowaddet crawled back to his side, this time being careful to stay out of range of his father's arms, should they start swinging again. He pulled his knife from its sheath and began to cut the knot he had tied in the bandage that was now cutting into the swollen leg. Gingerly, he unwound the soaked cloth to reveal the wound. It was oozing a thick yellow fluid. The smell made him gag. He turned his head away and spat on the ground, suppressing the urge to vomit.

Instinctively he knew he was smelling death. It had already taken hold of his father. He looked around him in despair. Panic welled up in his chest, making it hard to breathe. They were days from help and there was nothing he could do for him. He should have made him get into the lake last night. Maybe they could have soaked the sickness out. He should not have fallen asleep.

He cut another piece of cloth from his father's tunic and went to soak it in the lake. When he returned, his father was still not moving. The only sign he was still there was the rise and fall of his chest and the occasional soft moan.

Haddowaddet reached out and touched the leg near the wound. The skin was burning hot to the touch. He applied a little pressure with his fingertips and the foul liquid burst from the opening. His father moaned softly and rolled his head from side to side.

Using the dripping cloth, Haddowaddet washed away the caked filth from around the openings in his father's leg. He knew it wasn't much but perhaps it would help.

Sometime later, Baroodisick stirred and began to shout gibberish again. Haddowaddet could not make sense of any of it. He sat next to his father and cried softly. He thought of Gaboweete and wished she were here to sit with him.

He must have dozed off, for when he woke, the sun was peeking out over the distant hills that ringed the other side of the lake. He had slept all night. He turned to check on his father. He was still lying on the ground. Nothing moved. Haddowaddet stared at his chest. It was not moving either. He scrambled across the dry grass on his knees to his father's side. He nudged his arm and when he didn't get a response he began to shake him. Still, nothing.

He took his father's hand and held it up to his face. It was cold. There was no longer life there.

He sat quietly for just a moment, when quickly his sadness turned to anger.

"No, no," he yelled, while pounding on Baroodisick's chest. "You can't leave me. You're all I have left."

He sat cross legged on the ground next to his father and violently sobbed. The only witness to his passing were the flittering songbirds in the branches overhead.

Chapter 8
1740

It was over a week after his father had passed that he found his way home. He walked into camp emptyhanded with just the knife at his side. The only thing he had to remember his father by was the piece of red ribbon that he had always woven through his long braid. He had washed it in the lake and tied it around his wrist. It was old and faded, and even worn through in places, but it would serve as a reminder to Haddowaddet of all the good times they had together. He determined he would always keep it there.

When he walked into the clearing he did not bother to stop at their mamateek but went immediately to Gaboweete's.

He pushed aside the door covering, stooped, and stepped inside. As he straightened up, he realized neither her nor her family were there. It was obvious someone else had moved in.

"Where is Gaboweete?" he asked the old women that was bent over the cooking pot in the middle of the mamateek.

"Gaboweete?" she said in a thick raspy voice.

"Gaboweete. She lived here with her family when I left a couple of weeks ago."

"Oh."

"Where are they?"

"They left."

"Left for where?"

"Don't know. Coast, I guess."

"When?"

"Many days ago."

"Are you sure they went to the coast?"

"No. Not for sure"

In frustration, Haddowaddet backed out the door and let the stiff washawet skin slap back into place, hiding the old woman from his view.

He was stunned by what he had just heard. Gaboweete was all he had thought about since he had buried his father there by the side of the lake. He knew he had to return to her and ask her to be his wife. He knew his father would like that. Now he felt nothing but despair. She was gone and he had no idea where she was.

With his head bowed, he trudged back to the mamateek he had shared with his father. He was lost in his thoughts, not seeing anyone along his path, much less acknowledging the quiet greetings from those he passed on the way. He had to be alone to think, to decide what he would do next.

He entered the quiet mamateek that had not been lived in for over two weeks. He was glad no one had moved in while he was gone. He needed to be alone. He had no desire to talk to anyone except his father.

He started a fire and sat next to it, trying to remember anything she might have said to him that would give him some idea where she had gone. Try as he might, there was nothing he could think of that would help him.

He sat there staring into the fire for a long time, thinking and brooding over his losses.

He had watched his mother die when he was younger and now his father. He had no brothers or sisters. He had no one and no reason to stay here. The only thing left in his life was Gaboweete. He could think of no other purpose for going on.

He decided he would find her, whatever it took. Now, sure of his path, he relaxed and quickly fell into a deep slumber.

When he woke the next morning, it was with new purpose. He had dreamed about her again last night. He lay there in the early morning darkness listening to the songbirds and thinking about the dream he had the night before. He had found her sitting on a large boulder at the base of a waterfall. Her face had been upturned to catch the fine mist that drifted over her from the crashing water. A faint rainbow framed her in the bright sunshine. His heart leapt as he watched her there, completely unaware of his presence.

It wasn't the first time he'd had this dream and he wondered if it was telling him something. He wondered if this was the place he would find her. Perhaps his father's spirit was guiding him.

More light was filtering through the smoke-hole and he looked around at the home he had shared with his father. Everywhere he looked there were reminders of their time together; the hathemay and arrows protruding over the edge of the shelf, the second pair of moccasins standing in the corner, the cooking pot hanging above the fire, the loose feathers and partially finished arrowheads strewn around the floor. Each item triggered a memory and he felt tears trickling down his cheek. A sensation that had become all too familiar in the last few days.

With a deep sigh, he brushed away the tears and pushed back the covers. Outside, the familiar sounds of the awakening camp broke the spell. He pushed aside the door covering and stepped into the daylight.

During the morning, he wandered around the camp and talked with everyone to try and find out where Gaboweete's family had gone. From what he could gather, they had gone to the coast to trade with the Buggishaman. That made him a little nervous and anxious to get on the trail. He didn't like the idea of Gaboweete around any Buggishaman. They were unpredictable and couldn't be trusted. He hoped she was alright.

By noon he left the clearing with his hathemay slung over his back and a sheath of arrows at his side. In the pouch tied to his waist were some dried meat and powdered eggs given to him by members of the tribe, along with two fire starter stones. The knife tucked into his belt was the only other tool he carried. Some of the women stood and watched him leave. He heard one of them shout "Good luck, Haddowaddet," as he hurried down the trail.

It took him two days to reach the coast. He encountered two camps along the way. The band members reported seeing the family earlier that month, confirming that he was on the right trail. He knew now with conviction that he was going to find her. It made him feel better, more convinced that his ancestors were watching and guiding him. He spoke to them, thanking them as he walked along. Every step was taking him closer to Gaboweete. He imagined she was waiting for him at the waterfall from his dream, singing into the wind.

At the coast, he was faced with a fork in the road and there was nothing to guide him. The trail ended at the edge of the woods atop a hill that boasted an uninterrupted view of the sea. Both paths leading away, one to his left and the other to his right, were well travelled. He stood there for a few minutes looking out at the water. The waves were capped with white foam and he could hear them crashing against the base of the cliff down below. The mist was carried on the wind to where he stood. He sniffed the salt air, triggering memories of him and his mother long ago. He ran the tip of his tongue across his lips to taste the sea. He felt her there with him and he looked up at the sky and smiled.

"Where is she, mother?" he said aloud.

He heard nothing back, but in his spirit, he felt an assurance he would soon find her. She must be alright, he reasoned, or mother would not come to me like this.

He knew the coastline to the right would eventually lead him to the place where his mother had been killed by the Buggishaman. He hesitated, not wanting to see that place again, but it was the only place he knew there was a trading station. It was so long ago, everything probably had changed, he reasoned. That Buggishaman would probably be gone by now. He followed his instincts.

Another day's journey along the rugged and mostly uninhabited coastline brought him close to the trading post. The sun had set and it was growing dark. In the distance, he could see lights that must have been coming from a Buggishaman settlement. He decided to camp for the night and check it out at first light.

He awoke to sunlight on his face. He must have been tired, because he had slept late. The sun was over the horizon and climbing the sky. Quickly, he wolfed down his breakfast and headed to where he had seen the lights last night.

Following the path, he soon reached the clearing where the trading post had once been. A lot had changed since that terrible day so long ago. The tents had been replaced with wooden houses, many of them. The field where he watched his mother die was now fenced and sown with vegetables. It was hardly recognizable and he wasn't sure exactly where it had happened.

The beach was dotted with small boats, both in and out of the water, and Buggishaman were everywhere. A little off from the shore, a much larger boat floated in the deeper water. Some of the smaller boats were carrying things back and forth between it and the beach. The larger boat had long poles sticking straight up into the air with cloth wrapped around them that billowed in the wind. He wondered what they used them for. The boat seemed big enough to carry the entire tribe. He wondered where it was travelling and what it would be like to be on a boat like that. He would probably never know.

Close to where he remembered the trading tents had been, he spotted a group of Beothuk standing outside one of the wooden buildings. Colorful blankets were draped over the rail in front of the building and pots and pans hung from the ceiling over the covered porch, occasionally clanging together as they twirled on their anchoring strings. A Buggishaman with a long black beard stood in the midst of the group, holding the skin of a black washawet up to the sunlight, inspecting it for damage.

It was clear this was the new trading post.

He watched from a distance, wondering if he should go down there. He wasn't sure if it was the same Buggishaman. He couldn't tell from here and he didn't think he would recognize his face anyway. The eyes he would know. He was certain of that. A feeling of apprehension welled up in his chest. Even though it was so long ago, the picture of his mother lying on the ground was still very clear. He remembered how he had vowed to avenge her. For a moment, he considered going down there to kill him, if it was the same one. Then he remembered his father's council, and a vision of Gaboweete floated through his mind.

While he was mulling over the decision of whether or not to go to the trading station, he heard talking on the path behind him. Turning, he watched as a small group of women approached along the path he had taken to get here. They were carrying loads of animal skins on their backs, obviously heading for the trading post. More intent on their animated conversation, they did not notice him there until they were only a couple of bow lengths from where he stood in the shadow of a tall spruce tree. The two girls in the lead stopped and smiled at him with interest.

"Hello," he said.

"Hello," said one of the girls shyly.

"On your way to the trading post, I see."

"Yes."

"Do you live near here?"

"Yes, we do."

"We live in a camp just a little way upriver from here," added the second girl.

"I'm looking for someone," he said.

"Perhaps you have found her," said the second girl as she appraised him openly.

"Who?" asked the first girl, ignoring her companion.

"Her name is Gaboweete. She is travelling with her father and mother. I was told they were coming to the trading post."

"Gaboweete," she repeated, turning to the other girls who were all standing together listening to the conversation.

Haddowaddet's heart sunk as he watched them shake their heads.

"She would be about your age," he pressed. "She often wears yellow flowers in the tip of her braid. She loves to sing. She would have been here during the last month."

"No. We would have seen her if she came here."

"Are you sure?"

"Yes. We have lived here all summer."

With bitter disappointment, he turned to go. "Is there another trading post?" he asked as an afterthought.

"Yes, there is. It is on the coast, three days' travel back that way," the first girl replied pointing in the direction he had come. "It is smaller than this one but you won't have any trouble finding it. Maybe she went there."

"Maybe," he said and turned to walk away.

"Come back if you don't find her," piped up the second girl.

I should have turned left, he thought as he picked up the pace and hurried back along the trail. Why would mother have led him this way, he wondered.

It seemed the journey back was shorter. He supposed that was because he had hurried, even run in places. He felt Gaboweete was slipping further and further away from him. Already the leaves were beginning to fade into their fall coats with the light browns that in a few days would become blazing orange and red. He had to find her before winter set in, before the cold and snow kept him from travelling.

He arrived at the place where he had reached the coast the first time, just as it was getting dark. He found a sheltered place to sleep near the ashes of an old fire where someone had camped before.

After another restless, dream-filled sleep, he arose with the sun and took the left trail, where he hoped he would find Gaboweete. If the girls were right, it should take him two days to reach the trading post, maybe less if he pushed it.

With each hour that passed he felt a little more excited. He must be on the right trail now. He would see her again soon, and once again hear her sing. He smiled as he followed the worn path along the coastline. The clean salt air drifting in from the nearby beaches brought the scents of low tide. Overhead, seabirds wheeled and screeched in their unending search for scraps of food. He felt happy. Things were going to be good again.

Late in the afternoon of the first day, he spotted smoke from several campfires rising over the trees in the distance. A short while later, he walked into a small Beothuk camp on the banks of a river that flowed into the sea just a little downstream from where he stood. Two tapaithooks were pulled up on the grass not far from the three mamateeks. Looking at the width of the river, he knew that was the only way he was going to get across.

He walked to the cooking fire where it seemed most of the band had gathered for the evening meal. A tall young man rose to meet him as he approached the group, all of whom had been watching him since he entered the clearing.

"Join us brother," he said.

By now he was close enough to smell the cooking meat and the rumbling of his stomach reminded him he had not eaten all day. With appreciation, he dropped his hathemay and arrows and quickly crossed the space between them. They embraced in greeting and then returned to the fire. Haddowaddet found a spot on the ground next to the young man and gratefully accepted the meat that was held out to him. He tore off a sizable chunk with his teeth and chewed contentedly.

"What do they call you?" asked the old man sitting across from him on the other side of the fire.

"Haddowaddet," he murmured through the juicy piece of half-chewed meat. He swept his hand across his chin to wipe away the dribble that had escaped as he spoke.

"I am Joddofatt. This is my family," he said, sweeping his hand around the circle.

Haddowaddet nodded to each in acknowledgement.

"You are travelling alone," observed Joddofatt.

"Yes. I have no family."

"The Buggishaman?"

"Some of them."

"They will kill us all some day."

Haddowaddet nodded and sat in silence, savoring the warm meat.

"Where are you going?"

"I am looking for a woman."

"Is this *your* woman?"

"Not yet. But when I find her."

"Does she know this?" smiled Joddofatt.

"I think so."

"Why do you look for her here?"

"She is travelling with her family."

"Where were they going?"

"Trading post."

"There is one a day's journey on the other side of the river."

"Yes, I was told that. If they came this way they would have needed your tapaithook to cross the river."

"Yes. We have taken many across the river."

Haddowaddet drank from the container that had been passed to him, washing down the tasty meat.

"What is she called, this woman?"

"Gaboweete. Her mother and father would have been with her also."

"Gaboweete." He turned to the young man that had welcomed Haddowaddet. "Do you remember that name?"

"Yes, father. I took them across the river. She was the girl who sang. Remember her?"

"When?" asked Haddowaddet excitedly.

"Many days ago."

"Did they return?"

"No."

"I have to follow them. You must take me across the river."

"Not tonight. Tomorrow. It is too late now. You will stay here with us tonight."

Reluctantly, Haddowaddet nodded in agreement. Although he was anxious to get back on the trail, he knew there was no point travelling at night. Besides, these people were offering him hospitality and he did not want to seem ungrateful. Tomorrow was another day and he knew he was on the right trail this time.

With his feet pointed at the fire, he lay back on his elbows and gazed up at the twinkling lights in the dark sky. He wondered if she was also looking at the same lights right now. Two of those lights were his mother and father. He smiled into the night as he finished off his meat. Tomorrow was going to be a good day.

He was the only one awake at first light. He lay there for a moment, listening to the sounds of the forest stirring itself awake; the early-rise songbirds fluttering in the trees around the mamateek; the trees rustling their leaves, shaking off the remnants of last night's sleep; and the constant swish of the river that had lulled him asleep. He stretched and then quietly crawled through the sleeping bodies to the door. With one last look at his hosts, he pushed it aside and crawled through.

The morning had a chill to the air and a faint gray mist still floated just above the river. The surrounding hills were framed in pale yellow as, behind them, the sun began its slow lumbering climb into the sky.

He picked up his hathemay and arrows and walked down to the tapaithooks. At first, he had planned to wait until Joddofatt's son could take him across the river, but he was not yet awake and he didn't want to wait any longer. He had wasted too much time already.

Lifting one of the boats, he took it to the river and slid it into the water. He left it on the other side so they would be able to pick it up later.

By the time the sun had climbed to the middle of the sky he had put much of the trail behind him. Where the trail led him across open fields, he ran; where it wound through the forest, he maintained a fast walking pace. He felt every step was bringing them closer and he was excited. His mind was filled with pictures of her. His head was filled with the melodic tones of her voice. His heart was filled with an emptiness that he knew only she could fill.

Eventually his stomach began to remind him he hadn't eaten since last night. Through the trees that bordered the field he was crossing, he could see the blue water of the ocean. He turned off the trail and made his way down to the rocky beach. Standing on the large boulders, he could see clumps of mussels fastened to the rocks just below the waterline. He stripped off his clothes and waded into the chest-high water. It took a few deep breaths as he adjusted to the cold water. He didn't want to be in it any longer than necessary so he grabbed the shells by the handfuls, tore them from the rocks, and tossed them onto the beach.

Deciding he had enough, he scrambled from the chilly water and quickly pulled on his clothes. Soon he had a fire going and the mussels were cooking on the hot rocks around its edge. He scooped the hot, tender meat from the opened shells and ate until he had no room for any more. Although the day had a chill to it, the sun on his face and the rich seafood overtook him and he slept.

He awoke from the waterfall dream and looked around him. Realizing he had slept much of the afternoon away, he scrambled to his feet and hurried back to the trail. He was angry with himself. He had wasted all the time he had gained by running in the morning. How could he have been so careless. He rubbed his bare arms against the evening chill and began to run again. He would soon have to find shelter for the night.

It began to rain. In a matter of minutes, he was soaked and shivering with cold. Looking up at the dark angry sky he knew this was not going to be just a shower. Behind him, on the beach he had just left, the sky was split with a blazing flash of lightning, instantly followed with a crash of rolling thunder. It was close, too close. He ran off the trail toward a low hill that was formed by several large boulders, left behind by some ancient giant's hand. Instinctively he knew he must get away from the trees to escape the lightning. A gray fox dashed across the path in front of him, frightened by the pealing thunder. He lowered his head into the driving rain and quickly covered the remaining distance. He squeezed into a small opening between two of the boulders as the sky was once again lit with a streak of lightning and the earth shook with another loud crash of thunder. Loose soil drifted down on him from overhead.

All night the storm raged outside his tiny cave. There was no room to move around, barely enough to shelter him from the lashing rain. He just lay there, pressed against the cold musty earth, shivering in the darkness and wishing he could make a fire.

It was one of the longest nights of his life. He slept little and daybreak found him staring out from his temporary shelter into a morning of wind whipped rain under a gray and threatening sky.

He was freezing, so he pulled his thin damp cloak a little tighter around him. He was going to have to find warmer clothing than this. A few strides away at the edge of the woods, he could see a large tree lying on its side with faint smoke curling up from the jagged crack in the trunk where the lightning had struck during the night. He was happy he hadn't sheltered there.

His mind wandered back to Gaboweete and he decided it was time to go. He needed to walk to warm himself anyway. Fishing a piece of dried meat from his bag, he popped it in his mouth and then squeezed through the opening between the boulders and headed back to the trail.

By dark he had reached the settlement with the trading post. It sat at the mouth of a great river. Four of the Buggishaman's wooden shacks were clustered together near the shoreline. Like the last trading post, one of the buildings had bright colored cloth tied to a long pole in front of the wooden steps. That, he expected, was the trading post.

There was no one in sight. He needed a warm blanket, but he had nothing to trade for it. He needed information more, and he knew he would only get that from members of his tribe. He would have to wait for them to show up, hopefully tomorrow.

All the next day he sat in the shelter he built near the path, in sight of the settlement. It was another wet day, and although he had a fire, he was still cold and miserable. By late evening it was obvious no one was coming. He walked to the top of the small hill overlooking the settlement. The only sign of life was the thin lines of smoke drifting away from three of the buildings. There was none rising from the trading post.

There were blankets down there and he needed one. As the last light of the grey day slipped behind the hills, he began to make his way down the low slope, staying in the cover of the trees where he could.

He pulled his hathemay from his shoulder and carried it in his hand as he ran across the open field at a crouch, keeping low to the ground. He made it to the side of the trading post without being spotted. His heart was beating fast and the muscles of his legs were tight with tension. He knew if he were seen here, he would probably get shot by the Buggishaman, but he needed to get one of those blankets. The way things were going, it might get much colder before he found Gaboweete.

There were no lights in the dark sky and he carefully picked his way through the debris of wood that littered the ground. Someone had been cutting up firewood, splitting it, and stacking it against the wall at the back of the building, but had left much of it where it lay. His eyes were adjusting to the darkness, and by the time he reached the corner at the front of the building, he could make out the piece of colored cloth quietly fluttering in the light breeze. He stood there waiting, watching the other three buildings for movement until he was sure there was no one around. When he was satisfied, he moved again. The three wooden steps creaked loudly as he climbed them to reach the door. He froze on the top step and waited, listening, ready to run at the slightest sound. None came.

He placed the palm of his hand on the door and pushed. It didn't move. He gripped the wooden knob and pulled. It still did not open. This was taking too long. He nervously looked over his shoulder. Turning back, he noticed the small block of wood across the edge of the door just above his head. Reaching up his hand, he turned it away from the door edge and the door swung toward him. The wind caught it and he barely had time to grab it to keep it from crashing into the side of the building. In his haste, he stubbed his toe against a large rock as he lurched sideways.

With a stifled grunt of pain, he eased the door against the side of the building and slid the rock up against it. The cloud cover must have moved away because suddenly there was a large round moon overhead. The faint light from it filtered into the small crowded room. His ancestors must be helping him again, he thought. It made him feel a little more at ease and he looked to the sky at the twinkling lights. "Thank you," he said.

He stepped through the door and waited for his eyes to adjust again. He smiled into the darkness as he saw the treasure trove that surrounded him. All along one wall were shelves with jars filled with things he was sure he had never seen before, most of it just shapes, barely visible in the darkness. He wished he had more light.

A tiny window was centered in the end opposite where he stood, and along the wall on his left were piled boxes, blankets, and items of clothing.

He reached for one of the blankets and the steps creaked behind him. He froze, holding his breath, straining to hear any sound that was not a normal part of the night. Slowly, he turned his head and looked through the open door into the night, scared he would find a Buggishaman standing there. No one was there. He let his breath escape with relief.

He grabbed a blanket, and then a second one, and then stepped to the side lined with shelves. Reaching out for one of the jars he carefully stuck his fingers through the opening at the top. His fingers touched small round beads and impulsively he lifted it down and dumped the contents in his bag. That is for Gaboweete, he thought.

Many of the other jars were covered and he left them where they were. Further along the shelf his hand found a small hatchet. He tucked it into his belt and moved back to the door where he had dropped the blankets.

He took a last look around, knowing there was much more he could use, but he didn't want to load himself down. He still had to find Gaboweete.

Scooping up the blankets, he stepped through the door, jumped to the ground, and loped across the field into the night.

The next day he reached the first camp as he followed the well-travelled path paralleling the big river. He had walked all morning and entered the clearing at the midday. There were only two mamateeks and it appeared only one was occupied.

An old woman was cooking over a fire in the clearing and she turned to smile at him as he appeared before her. Her wide grin revealed a mouth of broken and missing teeth. Her face was creased and cracked with lines of age. Her eyes were hidden beneath the wispy strands of thin white hair that fell loosely over her forehead. As she straightened up as much as her old bones would allow, with one hand firmly gripping her side, it was obvious to Haddowaddet that time had taken much from her.

"Hello", she said cheerfully with only a thin sign in her voice of the pain she was feeling.

"Hello, old woman," he replied with respect.

"Come," she said, beckoning with her free hand. "Are you alone?"

"I am alone."

"You must eat with us. Riddoomon," she yelled toward the closed door of the mamateek behind her. "Come here. We have company."

Haddowaddet watched as a weathered hand appeared around the door skin and pushed it aside. The old man who stepped through the opening was also crouched and leaned on a stick he was clutching on his right side. Although there were red streaks in his hair where he had attempted to color it, it was obviously white underneath.

"Who are you?" he asked in a weak raspy voice.

"I am Haddowaddet, son of Baroodisick."

"Baroodisick. I know of him," he rasped.

"Come sit with us," he invited, as he shuffled to the fire where his wife was once again kneeling over the cook pot, stirring the thick mixture. Using the wooden stick, he eased himself onto a large stump. "You must tell us your news. We have not seen any of our tribe for a while."

"Oh," said Haddowaddet disappointedly. "I am looking for someone."

"Come. Sit here. Eat first and then we will talk," said the old man as he tapped the ground with his stick.

Although he was anxious, Haddowaddet remained quiet during the meal out of respect for his hosts.

"Who is this woman you seek?" asked Riddoomon as he licked the last of the stew from his fingers.

"Woman? How do you know it is a woman?"

Riddoomon grinned around the fingers in his mouth. "Even though I have lived many years, I remember the excitement of meeting the one. It is there in your voice; how you couldn't wait to finish eating. Now, tell us who she is?"

Haddowaddet grinned sheepishly. "Her name is Gaboweete," he said. She is travelling with her mother and father. She wears flowers in the end of her braid. She is a beautiful singer. They may have come this way during the last moon."

"I have heard her sing," said the old woman as she swiped her fingers around the inside of the pot to catch the last of the stew that was sticking to the sides.

Haddowaddet's breath caught. His heart leaped in his chest. He leaned in toward the woman, waiting for her to continue. He could feel the smile spreading over his face. From the corner of his eye, he could see old Riddoomon grinning widely.

"They were here a long time ago, at the beginning of the last moon, before the air turned cold," she continued. "Do you only have that blanket to keep you warm?"

"Where did they go?" he asked anxiously.

"You need a warm coat," she replied, ignoring his question. "The days are getting colder. Soon the snow will come."

"Where did they go?" he asked impatiently.

Disregarding his rising agitation, she continued, "I have a warm coat that might fit you. We don't have much meat. Do you think you can find a caribou for us? Riddoomon can't hunt well anymore and the winter is coming."

Realizing he was a prisoner to her information, he settled back to his original position. He knew he wasn't going to get anything else from her until she was ready, and she wouldn't be ready until she had what she wanted.

He couldn't disrespect their hospitality and just leave, besides, they obviously needed his help. This was going to set him back a couple of days, but then, they knew where Gaboweete and her family had gone, at least it seemed they did. He wondered if he could trust their information. She had effortlessly put him in a corner. She obviously knew what she was doing.

Chances were Gaboweete and her family had gone upriver but he couldn't be sure. In frustration, he decided he would get them a caribou. Actually, the old woman had decided it for him, he had just given in, since he really had little choice anyway. His mind was racing off in all directions.

"I will get you your caribou," he said finally.

"That will be good," said the old woman flashing her toothless grin."

Late the next evening he trudged into camp with a caribou slung over his shoulders. Inside the second mamateek, he tied its hind feet to the overhead poles and let it hang there. The old couple would carve it up from there.

Exhausted, he woofed down the meal the old woman had prepared for him. As soon as he finished, he returned to the other mamateek, lay down near the caribou and fell asleep. He wanted to make sure no animals got to the fresh caribou. Otherwise all the work he had done would be in vain.

Gaboweete came to him in a dream during the night and he awoke refreshed and eager to get back on the trail. He crawled to the door and lifted it aside to find the ground covered with a light sprinkling of snow. Shivering in the cold, he wrapped the extra blanket tightly around him and walked across to the other mamateek, leaving footprints as he passed. His breath swirled around his head as he hurried across the clearing.

Inside, the old woman had a fire going and was preparing breakfast. He huddled next to the fire and let its warmth wrap around him.

"Morning," she said. "Did you sleep well? Must have been cold."

"It was freezing, but I did sleep. I dreamed of Gaboweete again."

"You will soon find her. I'm sure of it."

"I hope so. It snowed last night."

"Winter is almost here. Perhaps you should spend it here with us. We could use your help."

Haddowaddet swallowed nervously. Was she not going to tell him which way Gaboweete had gone. She was a tricky old woman. He looked at her and shook his head, no.

"I have to find her. I can't wait through the winter. I must go now. Tell me where she went. The caribou will get you through if you spare it along. There is only two of you."

She looked at him and smiled, displaying the large gaps in her teeth, "I understand my son. You must go and find her. Young love," she said with a sigh. "Keep following the river inland. They planned to go all the way to the Great Lake for the winter. You will find her there. Your coat is over there," she pointed to a corner. "I adjusted it to fit you better. It will keep you warm. Thank you for helping us. We just might make it through another winter."

"Thank you. I will be leaving as soon as I eat."

"The caribou will help us get through this winter, although with that snow last night it seems we may have an early one. Here eat this."

He gratefully accepted the bowl she held out to him and made short work of the contents, wiping his mouth and chin with the back of his hand.

Riddoomon was still asleep on the other side of the fire. Haddowaddet expected he did a lot of that.

He wiped his hands in his pants, picked up the coat and slipped it on. "Good fit," he said. "Thank you. I hope you two do well." He bent and stepped through the door.

Standing there for a moment, he breathed deeply, filling his lungs with the cool crisp air, and then he picked up his things and started on the path that would bring him to Gaboweete.

He reached the falls the next day. The light snow had melted into the ground and the sun brought some warmth. It was a good day for travelling.

He heard the thunder long before he saw the mist rising in the distance. The sound stirred an excitement in him and he began to jog along the path. Like in his recurring dream, he expected to see her there on the beach below the falls. He ran the last few steps and pushed aside the low brush that grew along the shoreline beneath the falls. A sharp pain of disappointment pierced his chest as he discovered he was alone.

He stood there, absentmindedly staring at the water rushing over the edge, wondering what the dream meant. The way he remembered, the falls in his dream was exactly the same as this and he had never been here before. How could that be, he wondered. The picture must have been given to him by his ancestors.

Where was she?

Disheartened, he turned to take the trail. His heart leaped as he saw the tiny piece of red ribbon fluttering in the light breeze. He ran to the tree and pulled it free. It had to be her. It was the same as he used to tie his braid. It was the sign he had been looking for. She had been here. He crumpled it in his fist and punched the air in triumph.

"Gaboweete" he whispered, as he brought the crumpled ribbon to his nose and drew the scent deeply into his chest.

"Gaboweete," he shouted this time. "Gaboweete!"

His feet, as if controlling themselves, did a little victory dance amongst the loose stones of the beach. Sheepishly, he looked around to make sure he was alone. A broad grin spread across his face.

Seeing no one, he punched the air one last time with his fist before leaving the riverbank and returning to the trail. She knew he was coming. She knew.

The next morning, he woke to the sound of the whirling wind outside the abandoned mamateek he had taken shelter in last night. The fire had burnt itself out and it was bitterly cold inside. He pulled the blanket tighter around him as he lay there on the cold ground listening, watching his breath float upward in swirls of mist toward the smoke-hole in the roof. Through the small opening, he could see the swirling snow against the dark sky.

Reluctantly, he pushed the blanket aside and stoked the fire from the few embers buried in the ashes. He sat there next to it watching as it hungrily wrapped itself around the dry sticks he fed it.

He could tell from the wind that a storm was raging outside. He might not get to travel today. He reached into his bag and retrieved the piece of ribbon. Holding it in his hand, he imagined it tied to her hair. In his mind, he could hear her singing. It was a beautiful sound. The most beautiful sound he had ever heard. He wondered if she was thinking of him right at this moment. He wondered how much farther he had to go.

Chapter 9
1740

She had not wanted to leave. She wanted to wait for Haddowaddet to return. "He's only gone on a hunting trip. He'll be back in a few days," she had reasoned with her father. "Why do you need to leave so quickly for the trading post? A couple of days won't make any difference."

She had eventually beaten down her father's resolve and convinced him to wait an extra day. But in the end, Haddowaddet had not returned and she was obligated to leave with her family.

She remembered how upset she had been the day they left camp. It had been so long now, she wondered if she would ever see him again. He didn't even know where she was. What if something had happened to him that kept him from returning to camp when she had expected him to.

It was colder now, already the first snow had come. It seemed like it was going to be an early winter, and that meant a long one.

It was busy at the Great Lake. There were lots of people and there always seemed to be something to do. It was a nice feeling, having so many people around. For much of the year she and her mother and father had travelled around, first the coast and then along the Great River. They had met many of the tribe along the way but never stayed anywhere long. Her father had a wandering spirit her mother always said. Because of this, she had never made any lasting friendships. That was until she met Haddowaddet. That had been different.

She remembered the first time they met, how awkward he had been and how attractive that made him to her. They had only a few days together, but her heart told her he was the one she wanted. She had no doubt he felt the same way about her, even if he hadn't told her countless times.

She smiled as she thought of how he had gone out of his way to be near her in those few days. It had made her feel so good. No one had shown her that kind of attention before. She liked it. She didn't want it to end.

But that seemed so long ago now. Looking up at the darkening evening sky, she wondered if he was on his way. She hoped nothing bad had happened to him. She shuddered at the thought. She wondered why her mind kept going back to that.

Looking at the twinkling lights far overhead, she imagined he might be looking at the same lights right now. She hoped he wasn't all the way back at the coast. Winter was almost here. It would be much harder and more dangerous to travel in winter.

"Watch over him," she beseeched her ancestors. "Protect him from harm and bring him to me. Soon, please."

"What are you doing sitting out here in the cold?" she heard a voice ask.

Gaboweete looked over her shoulder at her mother, wrapped up in a blanket and standing on the snow-covered path. Behind her she could see the flicker of the campfire through the trees. It beckoned to her.

"I am talking to them, Mother," she pointed to the star-filled sky that spread over the quiet water of the Great Lake.

"And what are you asking them for?"

"Protection for him. I want them to bring him here safe to me."

"Come. Let's go back inside the mamateek where it is warm."

"Do you think he will come, Mother?"

"If it is meant to be he will come. That is the way it is."

"I wonder if he found the ribbon," she whispered to herself as she slid off the boulder and followed her mother back to the warmth of the mamateek.

It was two days since the wild snowstorm. It had appeared from nowhere, dropped a knee-high layer of snow over everything, and left as quickly as it came. Most of the snow had melted again but some of the larger drifts, like the one against the side of their mamateek, had stayed. Snow this early, she thought. We're in for a long winter.

She lifted the spoon to her nose and breathed in the warm aroma. As she returned the spoon to the pot and slowly stirred the thick stew, the door to the mamateek was pushed aside. Feeling the cold draft on her back, she turned to see who it was.

"Haddowaddet," she shrieked with joy.

The spoon slipped from her hand into the cooking pot. She scrambled to her feet, raced across the floor, and threw her arms around his neck.

He wrapped his arms around her, lifted her off her feet, and twirled her around, never letting his eyes leave hers. Setting her feet back on the ground, he tilted her chin and kissed her on the mouth, lingering there in the warmth of her response.

Slowly, the awareness that there was another person in the mamateek seeped into their consciousness and they broke their long embrace and turned back toward the fire where Gaboweete's mother sat silently watching them. A toothy smile split her face and wrinkled her weathered forehead.

"Well, aren't we the happy couple," she said.

Sheepishly they stood there, her arm around his waist, his draped around her shoulder, both afraid to let the other one go.

"Don't just stand there," she said. "Come and have something to eat. You look like you haven't eaten properly for days, Haddowaddet. You're skinny as a young spruce."

Taking him by the hand, Gaboweete led him to the fire and pulled him down to sit next to her.

Gratefully, he accepted the bowl of hot caribou stew her mother was holding out to him.

"Tell us all about where you have been and what you have seen," Gaboweete demanded eagerly. "Was your father upset with you leaving the camp?"

"I have much to tell," said Haddowaddet with a sigh. "But first, I have something to return to you."

Haddowaddet unfolded his free hand to reveal the crumpled red ribbon.

Gaboweete grabbed him around the neck again, spilling some of his stew. "I knew you would find it," she exclaimed excitedly. "I told you mother," she said, her eyes twinkling.

"Let him eat, girl."

The wedding was a joyous time of celebration. Everyone participated, from the youngest child to the most senior. The whole camp was abuzz with singing and laughter that carried on into the second day.

No one left the celebration hungry. It was a time to renew old acquaintances and make new ones, a time to share stories and good food, a time to cast away the cares and struggles of everyday life, a time to laugh and a time to dance.

Haddowaddet was overwhelmed with how everyone at the Great Lake accepted him and Gaboweete. It was as if they had lived there all their lives.

The sense of community was much greater than he had ever experienced. For most of his life it had been just him and his father, and for the most part they had kept to themselves after his mother died.

He knew this was going to be a safe place for him and Gaboweete to have a family, far away from the coast and the dangers of the Buggishaman. He was so glad he hadn't given up his search for Gaboweete.

Their wedding had taken place just a couple of weeks after he arrived. He barely had time to finish the necklace from the beads he took from the Buggishaman's trading post.

It hadn't left her neck since. He slipped his hand into hers and squeezed. He had never felt so happy.

Chapter 10
1755

Fifteen years had passed since he and Gaboweete had moved to the Great Lake. It seemed to Haddowaddet that the years had passed so quickly he may have missed some of them entirely. Life had become comfortable here. The community had grown larger over the years as more of the tribe moved away from the coast to avoid the unwanted contact with the Buggishaman. He and Gaboweete enjoyed these years. They made some great friends and they were involved in most everything that went on in the community. Life was good.

Most years he joined those of the tribe who made the trek downriver to the coast during the summer, to gather eggs and shellfish and to replenish the odemet. They went through a lot of odemet. There were so many people and so much to paint with it here at the Great Lake.

Gaboweete had only accompanied him once on the trips to the coast. She was content to stay in the camp with their son, Beeroute, who was born three years after they were married. He never felt concerned leaving his family at the Great Lake. There was always a large group at camp, and it was too far away from the coast to worry about the Buggishaman.

Beeroute was twelve now, almost a man. It was time for him to make the trip to the coast. Gaboweete had argued against it last year and he had given in, but this year he would be taking him. Gaboweete worried too much. What could possibly happen anyway, he thought. He always travelled with a large group.

Two days from now they would be leaving. He wanted to be sure he would be back for the birth of their second child, due to arrive when the leaves began to turned color. He wondered if it would be a girl this time. He thought he might like that. It had been so long since Beeroute was a baby, they had both thought they would not have any more. He did not want to be away when the baby came.

The group left the camp early, just as the sun was pushing itself over the top of the distant hills. There were seven of them; Haddowaddet, Beeroute, two other boys, and three men. It was early spring. Most of the ice had melted into the river and it was now a channel of angry rushing water, crashing over rocks and boulders and overflowing its banks in areas. At places the water was so noisy that conversation had to be shouted.

Beeroute was excited. He had never been to the coast before. He had heard many stories from his father and the other boys, and he was looking forward to seeing the ocean, and the monau (seal) and fish he'd heard so much about. He especially wanted to take the trip to Bird Islands. He was a little scared to go all that way in a tapaithook, but he wanted to see the island more. One of the boys with the group had made that trip last year, so Beeroute was grilling him with questions as they made their way along the wet, muddy trail.

"What's it like?"

"What?"

"The ocean?"

"It's huge, goes on forever. It's dark and deep and it never stops moving. Some say there is no bottom. There are great fish that live in the ocean. Many lengths greater than a tapaithook. When they are on the top of the ocean they spray water from their heads high into the air. Sometimes the waves are very tall. When the tapaithook drops to the bottom of the wave you can no longer see the land, only water everywhere."

"Wow, those must be tall waves," said Beeroute nervously.

"Don't worry, it can be scary at first, but you get used to it."

"How far is it to the island?"

"It's a long way. You can't see the island from land."

"How do they find it?"

"They just know where it is I guess."

"I wonder how they found it the first time."

"I don't know. Maybe they followed the birds."

"Maybe."

"There are so many birds, they are like a cloud when they fly up from the island. Their nests are everywhere. There is barely room to walk without stepping on one."

They had reached the falls and the roar of the water made further conversation impossible.

Beeroute looked at the falls in awe. He had never seen so much water. A mist billowed in a cloud from the river where the water fell. The mist glistened with colors each time the sun broke through the clouds.

He looked at his father and grinned.

Haddowaddet watched his son affectionately. He remembered his trek up the river when he was searching for Gaboweete and the wonder he had felt the first time he had seen the falls. Still, it was different to see it from his son's eyes. There was something magical and new to watch it in your child's eyes. It seemed to stir something deep in his chest. He knew this trip would have a lot of these moments for Beeroute. It was going to be a fun time.

His mind drifted back to the camp at the Great Lake and he wondered if the new baby would be a boy or girl. He hoped he made it back in time. Maybe this wasn't a good idea, to be taking this trip right now.

They travelled all that day, following the trail that wound through the woods along the river's edge. Just before dark, they set up camp for the night and had barely finished eating when the boys had fallen fast asleep, exhausted from the day's hike.

Haddowaddet sat near the fire with the other men, watching the boys sleep. Each man was lost in his own thoughts, comfortable in the silence.

Haddowaddet wondered what the future held for his young son. More and more stories were getting back to the Great Lake of clashes with the Buggishaman. They seemed to be building their wooden houses all along the coastline and taking the land wherever they pleased. Most of them had no desire to share with the Red Indians and defended themselves with their fire sticks that could kill a man at a great distance. Many had been killed by them in the past few years. The safest thing was to avoid contact with them and that was what he taught Beeroute. He hoped they didn't see any of them on this trip.

They had been walking all morning. It would soon be time to stop to eat. The sun, occasionally visible through the thick cloud cover, had crawled halfway to the centre of the sky. To the right, the river continued its unyielding rush to the sea. They were making their way through a section of the trail that was littered with waist high boulders. The boys were jumping from rock to rock rather than follow the lead of their fathers who were picking their way around them. As usual, they were making a challenge of it and jeering each other on.

Haddowaddet watched as Beeroute, encouraged by some of the others, took a run and leaped for a large boulder that was clearly out of his reach. Missing his mark, his foot slipped on the moss-covered side of the rock and dropped into the hole between two boulders. His leg twisted as he went down and he gave a sharp cry of pain.

Fearing the leg was broken, Haddowaddet ran to his son and lifted him from the hole. He lay him on the ground and felt the ankle as the others gathered around.

"Move your foot," he said to Beeroute, who was rolling his head back and forth and moaning in pain.

"It hurts too much," he said through clenched teeth.

"Do it."

Beeroute grimaced and gingerly wiggled his foot. With relief, Haddowaddet watched it move in a circle. Nothing was broken. There would certainly be swelling and bruising, but at least it wasn't broken. He reached into the hole and pulled out Beeroute's moccasin. The straps were busted.

"Well," said Haddowaddet, "I'll have plenty of time to fix that. Beeroute won't be walking on that foot for a day or two."

One of the other men helped him carry Beeroute beyond the field of boulders and sat him beneath the shelter of a large spruce tree. While the boys gathered firewood, the men built a lean-to. Haddowaddet started a fire near where Beeroute sat.

Once the shelter was built, the men packed up and they and the boys began their journey once again. Haddowaddet and Beeroute sat there watching the rest of the party walk down the trail on their way to the coast. Just before rounding the final bend and disappearing out of sight, Beeroute's friend turned and waved. He shouted something, but he was too far away and they couldn't understand, so he turned and disappeared with the others.

Two days later, Beeroute was hobbling around camp, using a short stick to take the weight off the swollen ankle. His father was cooking over the fire. A light drizzle was all that was left of the heavy rain of last night. The scent of damp earth was strong, carried by the light wind that swirled around him. He closed his eyes for a moment and drew the smell in. As he let the deep breath escape, he looked up at the gray sky. The blue patches in the distance were growing bigger. There was promise of a good day.

He wondered how his friends were doing. How could he have let this happen? The whole trip was spoiled because of that one careless act. Now he would have to wait for another year to make the trip to the Bird Islands. He wanted so much to see the ocean. Perhaps if he could walk soon father would at least take him as far as the coast. He as much as said that last night just before they fell asleep. Of course, that was after a lot of coaxing on his part.

Glancing down the trail, he was surprised to see his friend emerge from the trees and head up the path towards him. He seemed to be in a hurry.

"Look," he shouted over his shoulder to his father. "They are back."

"It's too soon," Haddowaddet replied. "They could not have gone to the Bird Islands and be back yet. And where are the others?"

Worriedly, he watched as the boy drew closer. Something didn't feel right. He stepped over to the lean-to, picked up his hathemay, and looked down the trail behind the boy, where it disappeared around a bend, watching for movement.

When the boy reached them, he slumped on the ground. He was breathing heavily as if he had been running. His shirt was soaked with blood. Streaks of dried blood mixed with dirt made a pattern across his cheeks.

He placed both hands over his face and began to cry uncontrollably, his whole body shaking.

Haddowaddet placed his hand on the boy's shoulder and shook him. "Stop crying and tell us what is wrong. Where is everyone? Look at me boy."

"They're gone. they're all gone," the boy blurted out between sobs and gasps for breath. His shoulders still trembled beneath Haddowaddet's hand.

"What do you mean? Where are they gone? What happened?"

"The Buggishaman. They killed them. All of them. They're all gone"

"Where?"

"On the river near the coast," he sobbed. "About a day from here."

"Are you sure they are all gone?"

"Yes, I'm sure. I saw it happen."

"Did the Buggishaman follow you?" Haddowaddet asked as he looked anxiously down the trail.

"No. They didn't know I was there. They didn't see me. They killed them all."

Leaning heavily on his stick, Beeroute stood there in shock, listening to his friend's answers. How could this have happened? How could they all be gone? He noticed his father repeatedly glancing down the trail and nervously scanning the woods around them.

"Where were you?" Haddowaddet asked the boy.

"I was in the woods gathering dry sticks for the fire when the shooting started," he sobbed. "At first, I didn't know what it was, so I started back to camp. Then I heard more of the loud bangs and anguished screams. I dropped the wood and began to run. When I got close enough I could see what was happening and I hid behind a thick bush. It was terrible."

"Why did the Buggishaman shoot?"

"We found one of their nets in the river and pulled it ashore. It was full of wasemook. We were cooking some of them to eat."

"How many Buggishaman were there?"

"I only saw two. I watched them shoot Father. He was the last one. He tried to shoot an arrow. This is his blood," he said, rubbing his hands over the stains on his shirt. He lifted his hands up to his face and stared at them. He stared at Haddowaddet. Beeroute could see the horror in his eyes.

"They rolled some of them in the river and laughed as they tumbled downstream. Then they sat there and ate the cooked wasemook. I had to wait a long time. I knew if I moved they would see me."

Haddowaddet slipped his arm around the boy's shoulder and held him tight against his chest as a fresh flow of tears burst from him.

"I held Father after they left," he sobbed.

"Should we go after the Buggishaman, Father?" asked Beeroute.

"No son. What could we do against their fire-sticks? Besides, you still can't walk without that stick."

"Maybe we could catch them while they are sleeping. There is only two of them. We must do something. They can't just do this and get away with it."

"I know, they deserve to die for what they did, but it is too risky for us. There have been enough of us killed for one day. We must go home."

Nanolute was born that day, but it would be another three days before he met his father and older brother.

Chapter 11
1774

Haddowaddet and Gaboweete were old but they were thankful they had lived long enough to see this day. Today their youngest son, Nanolute, would marry. Gaboweete had often dreamed of this day but never expected she would see it. Nanolute was a quiet boy, not outgoing like his big brother Beeroute; yet here he was getting married before Beeroute, who was 12 years older than him. Things seldom turn out how you think they will, but I'm sure Beeroute will find someone someday, she thought.

Manddilleeitt had captured Nanolute's heart. There was no doubt about that. Sweet Manddilleeitt. Since he first laid eyes on her two years ago, there was nothing else that interested him. He walked around with his head in the clouds and often did not see or hear anyone else.

As frustrating as it can be at times, it still brings me joy to watch, thought Gaboweete. I remember how Haddowaddet and I were. Look at what he went through to find me. She chuckled quietly to herself and snuggled her back a little closer to her sleeping husband.

In the darkness just before dawn, she contentedly watched her two boys sleeping. They were good boys, more than she could have asked for. They made her life happy and fulfilling.

They were different, yet the same in some ways. Beeroute had assumed the big brother role as soon as Nanolute was born. It seemed he had made it his job to protect his little brother and he took it seriously.

She remembered the day Nanolute came home with the makings of a black eye and bloodied nose, inflicted by one of the older boys because of some childish argument. Beeroute had stormed out of the mamateek in search of his brother's attacker. Later she learned some of the men had to pull them apart in fear that the other boy would not survive. Beeroute left marks on his face that never went away. No one bothered Nanolute after that day.

Because of their age difference, Nanolute and Beeroute had different circles of friends, but Beeroute still kept a close watch on his little brother.

Nanolute loved to listen to the campfire stories. He was content to sit for hours with the storytellers, asking them question after question as they repeated the history of the tribe. He wanted to know everything there was to know. Beeroute would rather be hunting or just shooting arrows at targets. He wanted to be outside roaming the woods, discovering the country.

It wasn't until the last few years, when the age difference didn't seem to matter, that they began to spend more time together. From then on, they were seldom apart. That was when Beeroute began to teach Nanolute how to hunt. He showed him which tracks belonged to each animal and how to have the patience to approach slowly and wait for the right moment before shooting. He taught him where to place the arrow to bring down a caribou, and the importance of not taking more than he could use. They spent hours together making arrows and discussing the best places to hunt. That was before Nanolute discovered Manddilleeitt, of course. Now he didn't have much time for anyone else in his life. It was Manddilleeitt and only Manddilleeitt.

As her mind wandered in the early morning darkness, Gaboweete wondered if she would have any grandchildren. She knew having little ones around again would make her happy. She knew Haddowaddet would love it too; he had an instant connection with children.

She noticed how he gave his attention to them rather than the other adults when they were around. He would often get down on their level on the ground and play their games. It was no wonder they were drawn to him.

She hoped the grandchildren came before long. Soon she would make the journey to Gossett with Haddowaddet, but she was content how things had turned out. She just wanted to hold them before she went.

She gave a little sigh as she fell back to sleep.

Later that morning, Gaboweete hummed to herself as she strolled the river path alone. Her only companions were the energetic songbirds, jostling for position on the branches around her. The dancing water of the river provided a soothing background noise to their constant chatter. Occasionally she joined them, breaking into song, testing her voice. Haddowaddet had made her promise to sing at the wedding. After much coaxing, she had finally given in. Her voice had aged as the years passed and sometimes cracked when she tried to reach some of the notes. It wasn't how it used to be. She wasn't sure she could even get through it, but they had all pushed her and she had to try.

Of course, Haddowaddet told her that her voice was great. That was Haddowaddet. He would tell her that anyway. "That voice can charm the birds out of the trees," he would say.

She knew she couldn't do that anymore, but it was still nice of him to say it.

She tried it again. Behind her, she heard someone clapping. There he was, back along the trail she had just walked, leaning his back against the trunk of a birch tree, one foot firmly planted on the ground and the other propped against the tree behind him. His face was creased with a wide grin as he vigorously applauded enthusiastically. His carefree pose flooded her head with memories of the younger Haddowaddet.

Smiling, she turned and walked back to him. There were many more lines carved there by the tireless hands of time, but it was the same face she remembered from the day he had appeared in the doorway of her parents' mamateek. The love that she had felt that day still burned strong in her heart. At first it had flared into a hot searing blaze at a look, or a touch, or some whispered word, but had eventually settled down to the persistent flame that had never flickered out.

They had made a great life together. They had a good family and today would welcome another into it. Her family had escaped conflict with the Buggishaman unlike many of the families who lived here at the Great Lake. She had lost no one when many of her friends had. She would be forever grateful for that. She was happy. When she reached the tree where he was standing she smiled into his eyes, slipped her hand in his, and led him back to the clearing where preparations for the wedding were in full swing.

Chapter 12
1777

Manddilleeitt stood just outside the doorway, watching little Shanadee crawl across the trampled grass of the clearing in front of their mamateek. She had spotted her father near the edge of the riverbank where he was busy fastening large sheets of birch rind to the frame of a tapaithook he was repairing, and she was determined to reach him. Her chubby bare bottom wiggled and swayed as she weaved in and out of the legs of the other children playing around her. Manddilleeitt smiled at the little squeals coming from her daughter as she got closer to Nanolute.

Seeing her approaching, Nanolute dropped to one knee and held out his arms toward her in encouragement. With a shout of delight, Shanadee scrambled forward, but her knees and arms got mixed up and she clumsily toppled over on her side. Her loud frustrated wail was cut short as her father's two strong hands scooped her up and lifted her naked sun-browned body over his head. He tossed her into the air and caught her as she fell. Shanadee giggled hysterically and Nanolute hugged her squirming little body close to his chest.

Laughing together, they made their way across the clearing and sat on the ground next to Manddilleeitt.

"She's crawling much better," said Nanolute proudly.

"It won't be long before she'll be waddling around behind you Nanolute. Then she will always be underfoot," replied Manddilleeitt, smiling at the pride on her husband's face.

By now, Shanadee had worked her way around behind her father and was hanging on to his long braid. Nanolute playfully swung his head from side to side, toppling her over each time she regained her grip. Her infectious laughter made both her parents smile with delight.

"I can't wait till I can take her hunting."

"That will be a while yet, Nanolute. She is a girl you know, and a little one at that."

"What's that got to do with it?"

"Nothing, I suppose, but you can't make her a boy if she isn't one." Manddilleeitt leaned her head back to let the warmth of the noonday sun wash over her face. She wondered if there would be a boy someday.

"She'll be able to hunt better than any of those boys," said Nanolute, his voice ringing with pride as he nodded toward the other children running around the clearing.

"Probably will if you got anything to do with it, my husband."

Nanolute smiled in agreement and sighed. "I've got to go to council tonight," he said reluctantly.

"What's happening?"

"We have to decide what happens to that woman they brought into camp."

"What's to decide? She was living with a Buggishaman trapper. You know our law. She can not be allowed to live. She has been contaminated by the Buggishaman."

"Is it really that simple Manddilleeitt?"

"It is the law."

"What if she was held against her will?"

"It doesn't matter. She can't live amongst us. That is the way it is."

"I don't know," muttered Nanolute softly as he reached around and pulled Shanadee onto his lap. "She's someone's daughter," he said as he buried his face in her mop of unruly hair.

The large mamateek was crowded and noisy when Nanolute entered. It seemed as if everyone was talking at the same time. He looked around at the sombre faces as he found a place to sit next to the other council members. Shortly after, the chief stood and held up his hands to silence the crowd.

"Quiet," he said, turning toward the door as two men entered, each holding one of the woman's arms. She shuffled along between them with her head bowed, her long hair covering her face. She still wore the dirty gray patched shirt of the Buggishaman, with its edges frayed and torn.

A murmur rippled through the crowd and the chief held up his hand again.

The three stopped in front of him and the council members who were seated on the ground behind him.

Nanolute glanced around at his fellow council members. He was the youngest of the group. He was surprised when he had been elected earlier this year, but he had been honored, if not a little nervous, to accept it. There had been a couple of meetings since but nothing as serious as this to deal with. He couldn't rid himself of the sense of dread he felt. He swallowed against the tension in his throat, wishing now he wasn't on the council.

The chief took his seat on the ground, leaving the woman and her guards standing. She cautiously lifted her head and looked around nervously. Her guards tightened their grip on her arms to keep her from bolting. Her gaze was fixed on the open door.

This was the first time Nanolute had seen her. He was surprised she was so young, probably his own age. He did not recognize her. She must be from one of the river bands, he thought.

"Tell us your story," commanded the chief.

Her frightened eyes flickered back and came to rest on the elder.

Everyone leaned toward her to hear her better. There was silence in the mamateek.

"He captured me," she said with a quivering voice. "I did nothing wrong. Why are you doing this?" A tear escaped and slowly trickled down her cheek.

"How long were you with him?"

"My mother and I became lost in a storm last winter. The Buggishaman found us, but it was too late for my mother. He brought me to his cabin and gave me food and warm clothes. Without it I would have died just like Mother. I had to stay with him. There was nowhere else for me to go."

"Did he lie with you?"

"Yes," she sobbed, dropping her head to look at the ground.

The chief looked to his council. "Do any of you have questions for her?"

"Yes," said one of the old men. "I have a question."

"Ask it then."

"Did you try to escape?" he questioned the girl.

The girl stared at him and shook her head. "There was nowhere to go," she said.

Nanolute was desperately trying to think of a way to get her out of this. He imagined if this were his little girl. "She was held against her will," he blurted out.

The girl lifted her head in search of the speaker. Her eyes found Nanolute's and he saw the desperate hope there.

The others looked at him thoughtfully. "You know the law, Nanolute," said one of them softly. "She has been contaminated by the Buggishaman. She must die or we will all be contaminated. It is the way of our people. We must protect our people."

Nanolute knew he was right, but his heart felt like it was in the tightening grip of some giant hand and he could barely force his chest to expand enough to draw in air. Defeated, he pulled his eyes away and stared at a spot on the ground in front of him.

The girl gave a whimper of despair.

The chief pushed to his feet. "As your chief, it is my responsibility to carry out this sentence," he said to the tribe, who were tightly packed into the mamateek to witness the hearing. "Bring her," he said to the two men who were supporting her as he strode out of the mamateek.

Later, Nanolute stood outside his mamateek door, watching the black smoke of the funeral pyre rise above the trees just beyond the clearing. His heart was heavy for the girl and he determined he would never let his Shanadee fall into the hands of the Buggishaman.

Chapter 13
1788

It was one of those crisp sunny winter days. The glare of the sun reflecting off the snow crust would momentarily blind you if you looked directly at it, yet the wind carried a penetrating chill that made you shiver.

He had been out all day with Shanadee. They had wandered the smaller ponds, where they had chopped holes through the ice and tried for fish, and now they were at Pond with Little Island. He knew they would catch fish in this one. They always did.

It was a good day, a fun day. They had many days like this before, and he cherished every one of them. It couldn't be much better than this, he thought, as he watched his daughter feed her line into the water through the hole he had hacked in the ice. Absentmindedly, he reached for the rabbit's foot hanging around his neck and rolled it through his fingers. He had worn it a long time. It gave him luck. Good luck.

It never ceased to amaze him how deep his feelings were for his firstborn. He had two boys as well now and he loved them, but there was a special bond with Shanadee. Since she was a toddler she had followed him everywhere.

He had watched her become one of the best shots in the camp with her hathemay. She could beat any of the boys when it came to placing her arrow on the target, whether it was moving or standing still.

They had spent long hours practicing, but that was part of the fun. She seemed to enjoy it as much as he did. She was usually the one who wanted to keep practicing, and he was happy to oblige. He knew she would grow up to be a strong independent woman in time. Someday she would find a good man and have a family of her own. That is the way of life, he thought. Of course, he would have to be a father-approved good man, and they weren't easy to find. But there was plenty of time for that. For now, he would enjoy these times with her. He smiled at the wanderings of his mind. I must be getting old, he chastised himself.

He looked at her with her head bent over the fishing hole, intently watching the line play out through her fingers as it was drawn under the ice. A warm feeling of pride filled his chest and he sighed contentedly.

He had taught her everything he knew about survival in this country, much of which he had learned from his brother Beeroute. He had been especially careful to keep her away from contact with the Buggishaman; nevertheless, he had told her over and over again to run if she ever encountered them. He was sure she would do that if she were ever in the situation. He hoped he would never have to find out.

He finished cleaning the second of the two fish they had caught and then laid them on the sled. As he turned back to the fishing hole he heard the telltale snap of a breaking branch from across the pond. He stood still, listening, as he nervously scanned the opposite shoreline. They were exposed here on the ice with no protection. It was probably an animal and nothing to worry about, but he wanted to be sure.

There. He was sure he saw movement.

"We have to go," he whispered urgently.

Squinting his eyes against the icy glare, he looked toward the sun and saw the outline of a man there at the edge of the trees. He had a gun. It was raised and pointed at them. Nanolute's blood ran cold.

Shanadee had seen the worried look on his face and dropped her line. She scrambled to her feet with her back to the Buggishaman.

Suddenly, something punched him hard in the chest, tossing him backward onto the ice. He gasped in pain as a thick curtain of darkness enveloped him, a darkness that would forever separate him from his beloved Shanadee. But in his last moments, as he struggled for air, he managed to spit out one last word to his daughter. "Run."

Part 2

Kirradittii's Family Tree

Kadimishuu & Ossaweet

Mokodihutt & Mammashoot

Thoowidgee & Odensook

Kirradittii

Chapter 14
1740

On the other side of the wall the wind howled in agitation, flinging the snow in all directions, creating a blanket so thick it would be impossible to see your hand in front of your face. There were no windows in this snow house and the walls were thick enough to muffle the sound, but Kadimishuu knew what was happening outside. He had seen the flurry of snow many times before. It was winter. It seemed as if it was always winter here in this frozen land. He sometimes wondered if the wind's anger came from having to spend time here in this cold, barren place. Often, he questioned why he stayed here himself. There were better places to live and raise a family. There had to be.

The dull glow emanating from the two candles of whale fat cast long flickering shadows over the glossy ceiling of smoke stained ice. Fat drops of melting water trickled down the curved ceiling until they were far enough from the heat to become ice once again. Three lumpy bundles of fur lay on the floor next to him. Underneath them were his two boys and Ossaweet, his wife.

His oldest, Mokodihutt, was born seven years ago, on a night much like this one. He smiled as he remembered the feeling of joy that had washed over him at the sound of his baby announcing his entry into the world. It was the best sound he had ever heard. At that moment, he had become a father. Seven years had not diminished the pleasure of that title, and now he had another boy to call him dad.

On that next morning, seven years ago, after the storm had spent itself, everyone from the village had come to see the newest member of the community. Kadimishuu had proudly shown off his tiny firstborn son amid the knowing smiles of the other parents. He still remembered how excited he had been that day. Somehow it had felt as if life had just begun. Everything seemed new. His little one totally depended on him to provide for him. It was both exciting and scary at the same time.

The village had accepted him and Ossaweet when they had arrived on their doorstep that year. They had been travelling toward a warmer place. The frozen land had no longer held any appeal for them and he had wanted to take his pregnant wife away from the cold. Initially he had planned to only stay the one winter, but that was seven years ago and they were still here. Now they were a part of the community as much as any of the S'kiemoos. They had helped him build his first snow house to replace the tattered tent he had brought with him. Without it they probably would not have survived that first winter.

Many times, he thought of leaving this land and continuing the journey to a warmer place. The S'kiemoos told him of the island where they went to gather food each year. They told him there were men who painted themselves red like him living there, and that the snow did not stay on the ground most of the year. They told him the waters were full of fish and the thick woods were full of animals to hunt. It sounded like a good place to live, but every year there seemed to be some reason not to go and it was always left to next year.

Last year Mokodihutt's little brother was born. He was very weak when he arrived and shortly after he had become very sick. He had been that way for most of the year, and he and Ossaweet had worried that their little boy would not make it. It had been a very difficult and scary time. Neither him nor Ossaweet had known what to do to help him. Thankfully, with the help of one of the S'kiemoo women's remedies, he had pulled through; but now it seemed it would be too difficult to travel with him. They feared he was not strong enough to take such a trip, even though the warmer weather would probably be better for him. Maybe next year. I'm getting too old now anyway, thought Kadimishuu. Life is not so bad here, he reasoned as he pulled the furs a little tighter around him, wincing a little at the pain from the open cracks on his fingertips.

He had gone out into the cold and wind again yesterday without the protection of his fur mitts. He knew the difference, but had done it anyway. His skin was so dry that exposing it to the cold wind always left him with cracks in his skin around his fingernails. He usually coated them in monau oil to protect them, but even that didn't help most of the time. He reached behind him and retrieved the container of paste one of the old women had given him and spread some of it over the sores. He wasn't sure what was in it, and it didn't smell the best, but it definitely sped up the healing process.

He settled back again and lay in the dim light listening to the muffled sound of the storm until his eyes grew heavy and finally fell shut.

Sometime later he awoke to the sound of barking and howling dogs. He could tell from the commotion something had happened in the village. Sled dogs did not act this way unless they were threatened or agitated about something.

He pulled on his heavy fur coat and mitts, grabbed his aaduth (spear), and crawled out through the low tunnel. He pushed away the new snow that had filled the doorway and squeezed out into bright sunlight.

Looking to his left, he immediately spotted the source of the racket. Close to where a group of dogs were tied up, several of the men were gathered around something lying in the snow. The dogs were still barking frantically. As Kadimishuu approached he could see dark patches in the trampled snow, and when one of the men moved aside he saw the still forms of two mangled dogs. His eyes followed the red snow a little farther along, where he found the crumpled body of one of the villagers. Everywhere he looked the snow was speckled red.

"What happened?" asked Kadimishuu.

"The great white washawet (bear) was here," announced one of the villagers.

"It killed them. All three of them," added another.

"See his tracks. He is a big one," said a third, pointing to the large imprints in the snow.

They all seemed to be talking at once as the nervous tension rippled through the little group.

Kadimishuu looked at the footprint. He had never seen one this big before. Nervously he glanced back at their snow house, looking for movement in the shadow cast by the sun.

"It is no longer safe here," someone said.

"No, it is not. It has the taste of our blood."

"It will be back for more. We have to hunt it before it decides to return."

"Was this during the storm?" asked Kadimishuu.

"No, the storm was over. See, they are not covered by snow."

"It probably happened at first light. He must have been out getting his dogs ready. Didn't see it coming, I'd guess."

"Over here," yelled a villager. "There are fresh tracks here in the snow. It went this way."

"Get your aaduths and hathemays. Let's go."

"Some of you stay here and protect the village, in case he comes back."

Kadimishuu took another look towards his snow house. He hoped his family was safe there. He turned back to the torn bodies of the sled dogs and he was afraid. This washawet was dangerous. It was a killer and it was big. He guessed it would take more than one arrow or aaduth to bring this one down.

They untied four of the dogs, led them to the washawet's trail, and let them run. The men loped along behind them in single file, their breath floating back over their heads like smoke in the quiet windless morning.

The dogs led them to a snow-covered beach that was ringed by cliffs encased in ice, rising to three or four times the height of a man. The water was hidden underneath the thick winter ice. The dogs were viciously barking at the entrance of a snow cave where the tracks of the washawet disappeared into the shadowy opening.

Kadimishuu looked around him. They had the washawet cornered. There was nowhere for it to go. The only means of escape would be through the men who were blocking its way to freedom.

Kadimishuu stood shoulder to shoulder with his fellow villagers. With their aaduths held out in front of them, they slowly advanced on the dark opening to the cave. The dogs were wild with the fever of the hunt and were making short rushes at the cave, skidding to a stop just short of the entrance. The noise bouncing off the icy surface was deafening. Inside his mitts, Kadimishuu's hands were sweating. The salty sweat was finding its way into the cracks in his fingers, stinging the open sores. Grimacing against the pain, he looked anxiously to his companions on the right and left. There were eight of them and the four dogs. That should be enough, he thought. A picture of his family asleep in the snow house flashed through his mind. The aaduth trembled in his hand. He hoped they could take this thing. He slowly released the breath he hadn't realized he'd been holding.

With the sun low on the horizon behind them they cast long shadows, almost reaching the entrance of the cave. The shadows were so much bigger than them. Somehow Kadimishuu found comfort in that.

Suddenly there came an ear-splitting roar from inside the cave, stopping the advance of the villagers in their tracks. With a rush, the washawet was out of the cave and amongst the dogs.

Something as big as that should not be able to move so fast, thought Kadimishuu. It spun in a circle, swatting at the snapping dogs until it connected with one who slipped on the ice and got too close. With a yelp of pain, the broken animal flew through the air, crashing against the ice-covered hillside. The dog slid down the slope until its lifeless body came to rest in the snow.

Kadimishuu tightened his two-handed grip on the aaduth and slowly moved toward the beast with the other men. They ringed the angry washawet in a half circle, aaduths held out in front of them. Behind the growling monster was the wall of ice. It had nowhere to go.

The remaining dogs continued to torment it, barking wildly and charging it in short bursts, distracting it from the men. The two villagers with hathemays placed their arrows into its front shoulder. The washawet reached back with its great mouth, gripped the arrows with its teeth and snapped them off like pieces of dried grass. The first aaduth was plunged into its side behind its front leg. It reared up on its hind legs with a roar of rage, swinging its head from side to side, searching for this new source of pain.

The great white washawet towered over Kadimishuu, and he looked up at it in fear. He had never encountered such a beast. He wanted to turn and run. The other men's aaduths were plunged into the flailing animal and Kadimishuu added his. When he tried to pull it back to use it again the washawet twisted, yanking it from one hand. He tried to hang onto it with the other and didn't see the paw coming. It caught him with a glancing blow, raking his face with the fully extended talons and throwing him backwards on the ice.

He lay there dazed and confused. He could still hear the commotion but everything was spinning and clouded. He closed his eyes just for a minute, he thought. He knew he shouldn't sleep, but he was so tired.

He opened his eyes again. His sight was clearer now. He was staring at a clear blue sky. One of the villagers was staring down at him, gently shaking his shoulder.

"Are you alright, Kadimishuu?" he asked.

"He's alive. Just shaken up," said another.

"Look at his face. What a mess."

"We'd better get him back. Get that taken care of."

Kadimishuu put his hand up to his face; he could feel the torn flesh. When he took his hand away it was covered with fresh blood.

He remembered the washawet. "Where is it?" he asked, anxiously looking up at the faces of the villagers standing in a circle around him.

"What did he say?"

"Not sure. Can't understand him with that hole in his face. Besides he's talking with his old Beothuk words. I think he's worried about the washawet."

"Don't try to talk, Kadimishuu. You are just making it bleed more. Keep this cloth against your face. The washawet is dead. You're ok. We have to get you back to the village to get that gash taken care of."

"Can you walk?"

Kadimishuu nodded and pushed to his feet with the help of two of the men. The ground spun before his eyes as he shuffled along with the help of his fellow villagers on each side.

Chapter 15
1745

They had almost finished the evening meal that Ossaweet had prepared for them. Soon it would be time to sleep.

"Some of the villagers are planning the annual trip down to the island," said Mokodihutt casually.

Kadimishuu glanced at Ossaweet. He saw her shoulders go rigid as she spooned out the last of the food from the meal pot. He'd expected this was coming. They'd had this discussion last year and had been able to convince Mokodihutt he was too young. He didn't think Ossaweet would win the argument again.

"I want to go," he announced.

"No," said Ossaweet, a little too quickly.

"Why not?"

"It's too far, it takes too long, and it's too dangerous. That's why not."

"I'm old enough, mother. The villagers have done this many times before. There is no danger. Tell her, Father. I want to see other Red Indians. I want to see where they live."

Kadimishuu kept his eyes on the soup he was drinking. He understood his wife's concerns, and in fact shared some of them, but Mokodihutt was twelve. It was time he joined the hunt; to do something his father had never done. After all, isn't that what you want for your children, to experience things you haven't?

"Father?"

He met his son's pleading eyes and felt the little resolve he had melt away.

"I think he should go," he said. "It's not really all that dangerous. Those villagers are good men. I know them. They will look after him. It will be good for him. He'll be back again before the winter sets in."

He looked at Ossaweet and saw the pained resignation in her eyes. He also saw the stray tear slip from the corner of her eye and trickle down her weather lined face.

"I'm scared," she whispered softly.

Kadimishuu slipped his arm around her shoulder and pulled her head against his chest. "It will be okay. We will have a long winter to listen to his stories when he returns."

A week later, the small group left the village. There was one other boy, but he was four years older than Mokodihutt and he had made the trip before. The four other men had all made this trip before as well. That made Kadimishuu feel more comfortable.

It was the month of Bedejamish bewajowite (May), summer was close. The wind did not have the same chill; some days it was possible to detect a faint warmth, a promise of things to come. Out in the bay the ice was melting and breaking up. Farther off shore he could see open water and large icebergs taking their slow journey southwards, a journey he at one time thought he would take. At least his son would get to do it.

Ossaweet stood on the frozen shore and watched them push the boat across the thin ice until they reached the open water. With her arms wrapped tightly around her she anxiously stood there while they clambered aboard the boat and pushed away from the edge of the broken ice. She had to be sure her boy made it out okay. She had an aching emptiness that was growing inside her. She feared she might never see her son again. She should never have agreed to this. He was too young. He was just a boy. What was she thinking?

Kadimishuu watched from outside their mamateek that now stood in place of the melting snow house. He felt good for his son. He was almost a man and this trip would get him there. He smiled as he watched the boat move out of sight beyond the point. Mokodihutt would have a good time he was sure of it. A small part of him wished he could have gone with him. He had never been down to the island, probably never would now. Maybe the warmer weather would be good for all these pains in my joints, he thought.

Mokodihutt sat in the back of the boat. He took deep breaths, filling his lungs with the salty air. He liked the taste of the drops of spray on his lips. He was excited. He had never been away from home like this before. He listened to the conversation of the villagers. They had lived in the village long enough that his family had learned the language, in fact, now they used it much more than their own.

Just before they rounded the point, he took one last look over his shoulder at the lonely of his mother standing on the beach. He could see his father farther back, next to the mamateek. His brother was nowhere to be seen. Probably inside, he supposed. He hated to be out in the cold.

Mokodihutt wanted to wave but he didn't want the others in the boat to think he was still a boy. He turned back and stared ahead, swallowing hard to fight the sadness that sought to overwhelm him. The only sound, other than the low conversation, was the occasional snapping of the sail in the light breeze and the waves lapping up against the edge of the pack ice and the sides of the small wooden boat. It was peaceful and there was little to do other than watch the land slowly crawl past.

Much of it was still blanketed in snow and ice, but here and there the ragged face of the cliffs was visible where the ice had fallen away, tumbling into the cold water below. Short barren trees could be seen at the top, pushing their bare limbs through the snow, reaching toward the sun that would soon restore their covering of leaves. The land looked lonely and deserted from this viewpoint. He wondered why his father had picked this place to live. He pulled his fur hood a little tighter around his face.

By late afternoon they found themselves in a field of thicker pack ice and had to take the sail down to slow their speed, for fear of hitting one of the ice pans. As darkness approached, the land disappeared behind them and they found a large floating ice pan to pull the boat up on for the night.

They made a small fire to warm their food, ate mostly in silence, and then huddled together underneath the sail on the leeward side of the boat. Soon the only sound Mokodihutt could hear was the whistle of the night wind occasionally accompanied by the snores from his fellow travelers.

He was still too excited about this trip to sleep. He thought of his family he had left back at the village. He wondered how his mother was doing. She was probably staring at the ceiling of the mamateek right now, too worried to sleep. He wondered about his little brother. He never seemed to be well, always fighting a cold or something else. It wasn't a good place for him to be living.

As the night tugged back the covers and the cold gray dawn began to appear, Mokodihutt opened his eyes. He was cramped and sore from the ribs of the boat he had slept on all night. Most of the men had chosen the ice pan rather than the uncomfortable boat. Only he and the other boy had slept inside it.

Even though he had slept under thick furs, his fingers and toes were tingling with the cold and he wriggled them to warm them up. His breath hung in front of his face in a thin cloud.

Peering over the side, he saw dark water all around the ice island. Although there was some pack ice, it had thinned out and they floated alone. He could feel the gentle rocking motion of the ice they were on as the sea pushed them slowly along.

There was no sight of land anywhere.

He watched the oldest villager of the group standing some distance from the rest. Cupping his hands around his eyes, he stared up at the sky where a few gray clouds slowly drifted along and then back at the path they had made through the water.

"Getting his bearings," said one of the men, noticing the direction of Mokodihutt's gaze. "He's one of the best. Don't know how he does it, but he will put us in the same spot we landed last year."

Mokodihutt thought he would like to learn how to do that. He determined he would ask the old man when he got a chance. That would be a pretty amazing thing to be able to do.

Eventually the old man walked back to the others and announced, "It's time to get the boat back in the water. We are drifting away from the island and need to get back on course."

Once they had launched the boat, they raised the sail and the old man took up position in the stern next to Mokodihutt and took a firm hold on the tiller.

"How'd you do that back there?" he asked the old man.

"Do what, son?"

"Find the way with no land in sight?"

"I don't know. I just look up there to our ancestors and they show me the way. They put something here in my head and I just know which way is the right way to go. It's a feeling."

"Is that why you cup your hands?"

"If it is not dark enough I have to do that to see the lights up there."

Mokodihutt thought for a while and then asked, "Are your ancestors up there too?"

"Yes, our ancestors are there with yours."

"Can I learn how to do that?" asked Mokodihutt.

"Maybe. Can you find your way around the woods?"

"Yes."

"That's a start."

Mokodihutt looked at him expectantly.

The old man continued to stare ahead of the boat as if he could see the place they needed to be, somewhere out there in the distance.

Finally, he said, "The lights of our ancestors are arranged in a certain order up there. They are each given a place when they get there. You have to learn the pattern from each place you stand."

"I will teach you," the old man continued, "When it is dark and you can clearly see the lights."

"Good, I want to learn."

By mid-morning they once again encountered thick pack ice, but far in the distance they could see the pale blue outline of land, just above the edge of the water. The sail was shipped and they began to row through the field. Those who weren't rowing used long sticks to fend off the floating pieces of ice. Deeper into the field, Mokodihutt could see the dark figures of monau scattered over the floating pans.

As they got closer, two of the villagers grabbed their clubs and jumped to the nearest pan. They quickly made their way to the monau, clubbed one each and dragged them back to the boat. They cleaned them on the ice, cut slabs of the oily liver and heart and passed it around. The warm, fresh meat was delicious, a welcome change from the dried meat they had been eating since they left the village. It was the first time Mokodihutt had eaten it this fresh. He liked the oily taste.

The two carcasses were heaved into the boat and the men clambered back in after them. The boat was pushed away from the ice and they got underway again. It seemed everyone's spirits had been lifted with the fresh meat. There was much more talking going on, Mokodihutt noticed.

Before long it began to blow. With the wind came driving snow, making it difficult to see. Now the sea was building and pushing the ice around much more vigorously. The boat was in danger of being crushed by the cresting waves and constantly moving ice. It was getting harder to fend it off and several large pieces already smashed into the exposed sides of the boat.

"We have to find a large pan to pull the boat up on and ride this out," shouted the old man as he scanned the field. "There," he shouted above the wind. "We'll make our way over to that one."

Mokodihutt looked in the direction he was pointing. Shielding his eyes against the driving snow, he could see a high peak where the ice pushed up out of the water. It was close.

They maneuvered the boat through the drift ice, next to the berg. The howling wind made it hard to hear, so little was being said. The sea was washing up against the rock-hard walls, tossing smaller pans against it and threatening to do the same with the boat and its crew. Using their oars and poles, they managed to push around to the lee side where the iceberg flattened out into a large plateau that sloped down towards the water. With the aid of the waves, they were able to run the boat up the slope where several of them jumped out and dragged it away from the water's edge.

Everyone jumped out onto the ice. They were in the shelter of the high peak and the wind was much quieter on this side. Mokodihutt and the old man grabbed the end of the long rope attached to the front of the boat and walked until it came tight.

The others manned the sides of the boat. Together they began to pull it further up the slope to make sure it was safely out of reach of the waves.

Mokodihutt had his back to the boat, straining against the rope draped over his shoulder. He felt the island lurch, followed by a loud crack that echoed above the shrieking wind. He was momentarily pulled off his feet and the rope was jerked from his hands. He turned in time to see the large crack that had opened in the ice directly beneath the boat. In horror, he watched the gap widen and the boat and everyone in it tumble into the gaping hole. The large section of broken ice sheared off, reared up in the water as it rolled, and then came crashing back on top of everyone and everything that was in the water. Chips of ice showered over Mokodihutt and the old man as the broken section ground against the larger berg. The moan of grinding ice filled Mokodihutt's ears; a sound he would not soon forget.

Mokodihutt lay there on the ice beside the old man in stunned silence. There was no sound but the wind whistling through the peak behind them. After the initial lurch, their section of the berg had barely moved. The snow still swirled around them, slowly covering a single mitten lying at the edge of the cracked ice. It was the only sign the others had been there.

It had all happened so fast. There had hardly been time to take a breath.

"Are they gone?" he asked with a trembling voice.

The old man nodded. "Yes son, they are gone. There is nothing we can do for them now. And we have lost the boat with all our food and all our tools."

At first the old man's words did not register. He just sat there in shock from what he had just seen. They were all gone, just as quick as that. He had never seen death up close like that before. He began to sob.

The old man sat next to him and slipped his arm around his shoulder. "It's alright," he said. "You need to cry for them. It is the only way to get release from this. They were all my friends. I knew most of them since they were born."

Mokodihutt sobbed quietly as they sat there in silence, the falling snow slowly covering them as they drifted through the heaving sea.

He awoke the next morning to the bright sun on his face, but he was shivering from the cold. The sun wasn't providing much heat, but it was much better than the driving wind and snow they had fallen to sleep with. The covering snow had probably saved them from freezing last night as they lay huddled together on the ice.

The old man was not yet awake, but he could hear him breathing heavily. He pushed to his feet, brushed off the snow, and looked around. The land they had spotted yesterday was much closer now. The storm had pushed them toward the shore. All around, the sea was spotted with pieces of floating ice, but the gaps of open water were too big for them to make it to shore. They were stuck here on this floating island.

He watched for a while as the rocky coastline slowly passed them by. The land looked much the same as what they had left. There were perhaps a few more stunted trees, but that was all. There was no sign of life there, but then maybe he would not see it from this distance. He wondered if this was where his people lived.

He stood there a long time staring at the land, searching for movement, but saw none. Then he realized where he was standing and the hopelessness of their situation began to sink in. He felt a tightness inside his chest and his throat went dry. He was scared. They had no food, no shelter, and no way to get off this ice. Perhaps it would have been better if they had gone with the others, he thought.

Pictures of his parents and his little brother, Kassussabook, drifted into his mind. Now he wished he had never come on this trip. He wished he could see them again. Chances were he never would. He felt sick. He thought he might lose what little was in his stomach.

His thoughts were interrupted as the old man stirred behind him. He glanced over his shoulder to see him clumsily push to his feet.

"Everything has stiffened up, boy," mumbled the old man with a groan.

Mokodihutt held out his hand to steady him, but the old man brushed it off.

"I'm alright."

"What are we going to do?" asked Mokodihutt anxiously, still feeling a faint churning in the pit of his stomach.

"First, we are going to eat," said the old man with a grin. "Can't think on an empty stomach."

"Eat? Eat what?"

"This," said the old man. He slid his shoulder bag around to his front and lifted the flap.

Mokodihutt had not noticed it before. He had lost his own with the boat.

Still grinning, the old man pulled out a bundle wrapped in monau skin. He unfolded it to reveal two large slabs of dried meat. Mokodihutt's mouth filled with saliva and the rumble in his belly now turned to hunger.

"Here," said the old man, tearing off a piece. "Have your breakfast."

Mokodihutt thought he had never tasted anything so good. He felt the old man watching him and he glanced up to see him smiling.

"What do we do now?" he asked, around the large lump of meat that partially filled his mouth.

"Well for one thing, we must spare this along," he said, wrapping the rest of the meat and slipping it back into his bag. "We don't know how long we will be out here on this piece of ice."

"But, how are we getting off it?"

"Don't know that yet. Just have to wait and see, I guess. At least the wind and snow has stopped, and look at that sun. That makes it better."

"We are closer to the land," said Mokodihutt, feeling a little more optimistic.

"Perhaps we should have a look around. Maybe there is a cave or something where we can get more shelter if we have to sleep here again tonight."

Mokodihutt followed him as they made their way up the gentle slope to the base of the peak that thrust up from the middle of the island. The going was slow at first as the old man walked the stiffness out of his legs. Mokodihutt watched him from behind.

He felt a lot better having him here. He felt like maybe they might find a way to get off this island. If there was a way, the old man would find it.

Once they reached the base of the peak they began to circle it, looking for openings as they went.

"Here we go," said the old man who was a little ahead of Mokodihutt. "This will do just fine."

Catching up to him, he saw what the old man was looking at. A shallow opening had been formed in the side of the peak. It was small but still big enough for them both. It would be much better than sleeping out in the open like last night.

He looked toward the land. The view was much better from up here. Now he could see farther behind the coast. Somehow it seemed closer.

The sun was finally beginning to thaw him out, he had food in his belly, and he wasn't alone. Things felt much better than they had when he woke earlier this morning. Maybe it would be alright after all.

They continued around the peak until they could go no further. Their way was blocked by a sheer wall of ice that dropped away to the sea below; it's base was smooth and shiny with the constant washing of the waves. Mokodihutt pushed back from the edge. The dark water reminded him of the others. He shivered at the memory.

They turned around and went back the way they had come. The small ice cave was the only shelter on the island.

It took three of Mokodihutt's strides to reach the back of the cave. The old man had to stoop to avoid hitting his head on the low ceiling that sloped down at the back. Against the back wall of the cave they found evidence they had not been the first to use it. Small bones were scattered around, some melted into the floor.

"Must have been a washawet," declared the old man. "Didn't leave us much," he said as he picked up one of the bones and stuck the end in his mouth.

"Think he's still around?" asked Mokodihutt, worriedly glancing at the opening.

"Long gone. These bones have been here forever. Nothing to worry about. We're safe enough here. Besides, if he comes back we will eat him."

Mokodihutt looked up in disbelief and caught the mischievous smile on the old man's face. He laughed aloud. For a moment, he thought he wouldn't be able to stop laughing. He wasn't sure why he found it so funny, but he did.

He was glad he wasn't stuck here alone.

"I told your father I would watch over you and that's what I intend to do."

Mokodihutt smiled at him appreciatively.

All that day, as the ice lumbered along on its journey south, they watched the coast slip by from their rear facing viewpoint. Mostly they passed tall barren rock with random patches of snow in areas where the sun's warmth had not yet penetrated, but in some places, small twisted trees grew down to the water's edge. In some places, they drifted closer to the land where it jutted out into the sea, but even then it was too far away to reach.

As night approached, they shared some more of the dried caribou and then huddled together on the floor at the back of the cave until sleep overcame them.

Mokodihutt dreamt that night.

In his dream, he was back in the snow house in the village. His mother, little brother, and father were all there. They were laughing. It was a happy time. He watched his father rub the scar on his face as he was often prone to do. It seemed to remind him of that day and he began to tell the story of the washawet once again.

Mokodihutt woke before dawn. Through the opening he could see the many twinkling lights in the sky overhead. He lay there in the cold thinking about home. He wondered if he would ever see his family again. They would always wonder what had happened to him and the other villagers. They would probably never know. The sadness of it all settled over him like a dark cloud and the tears began to trickle out of the corner of his eyes.

He had wanted to take this trip for the adventure. Never had he dreamed it would go this way. They had lost everything and now it was only a matter of waiting to die. It wouldn't be long before the dried meat would be gone and then that would be it. He wondered what it would be like. He supposed someday someone would find them in their ice cave and wonder who they were and where they had come from.

"Can't sleep?" he heard whispered from the darkness next to him.

Hurriedly he brushed the tears aside. "No," he replied.

"Thinking about back home, are you?"

"Yes. I had a dream."

"Tell me about it."

"It's nothing. I was just back in the village with my family."

"Bet it was warm there," said the old man as he pushed to a sitting position with his back against the wall of ice. He began to vigorously rub his hands together and stamp his feet. It was light enough now to see the plume of vapor floating above his head, each time he blew out his breath. Mokodihutt noticed he was shivering himself. He stood and began to walk around the small enclosure.

"Hope it's sunny today."

Mokodihutt kept circling.

"We have to go outside soon."

"Why?"

"We have to keep watch for boats; someone to help us."

"Do you think anyone will come?"

"Sure. The farther we drift south the more people there will be. Here, have some more of this dried meat."

"Do you think it will be my people?"

"Could be. Might be white men too. Doesn't matter, as long as we get off this floating island of ice."

"Hope you're right."

"I am."

They watched the water all morning and saw nothing other than floating ice and a barren vacant shoreline in the distance. By mid afternoon Mokodihutt stopped looking and sat on the ice, dejectedly watching the old man pace around their island.

He was hungry and he was cold, despite the sun. This was hopeless. What was the point. The old man was wrong. They weren't going to get off this ice, ever.

"Look," shouted the old man, pointing excitedly toward the coast.

Mokodihutt jumped to his feet and looked in the direction he was pointing.

They were approaching a long point of land that jutted far out into the water. At the edge of the trees he could see movement. He shaded his eyes from the glare of the ice and figures came into focus. It was two men carrying a boat. He thought they might be Indian men.

Mokodihutt began to jump up and down and wave his arms frantically.

"Help us, help us," he yelled across the water.

At first it seemed they didn't hear him. He yelled again and began to run back and forth across the ice.

The men stopped walking and looked his way. They just stood there staring at them, not making a move to help.

"What's wrong?" he shouted to the old man. "Why aren't they coming?"

"Maybe you should try your own language. They don't understand what you are saying."

"Oh yeah," said Mokodihutt sheepishly. "I forgot. I've been speaking yours for so long."

He tried yelling again. This time in Beothuk.

The men waved back. Then they launched their boat and headed in their direction, picking their way through the small ice pans that littered the bay.

"They may not want to take me," said the old man.

"Why not?"

"Our people have fought yours in the past."

"Guess its my turn to watch out for you," Mokodihutt said over his shoulder, as he watched the tapaithook approach.

He had heard stories about this boat but this was the first time he had seen one. It looked flimsy, like it could tip over at the slightest movement.

As the tapaithook drew closer, his eyes were drawn to the two men. The one in the back was paddling the tapaithook with strong powerful thrusts. His long hair was tied in a single braid that hung to his waist. The younger of the two sat in the front with a hathemay held across the boat by his waist. Between the fingers of his free hand dangled a single arrow. What interested Mokodihutt was their faces. They were both painted a dark red. These are my people, he thought excitedly.

He noticed the man in the front was watching the old man suspiciously. The tapaithook bumped gently against the ice.

"Its alright," said Mokodihutt. "He means you no harm. He's my friend."

The Beothuk looked at him curiously. "How do you know our language? You look like a S'kiemoo."

"I am Beothuk. We are travelling together. We live in the same village." He pulled down his hood.

The Beothuk looked at each other.

"Is that why you are dressed like him?"

"Yes."

"How did you get here?"

Mokodihutt proceeded to tell them what had happened as they pulled their tapaithook up on the ice.

"We have little food and no water. We lost everything," said Mokodihutt.

"We have a monau back there," he pointed to the beach. "You can eat with us."

The old man eyed the tapaithook suspiciously. "We are not getting in that," he said to Mokodihutt. "That's not safe."

"What did he say?" asked the older of the two Beothuk.

"He says he can't get in the tapaithook."

The older Beothuk shrugged his shoulders. "That's up to him. He can wait for someone else to come along," he laughed to his companion. "What about you?"

"I'm going ashore with you. He'll come too."

"Let's go."

"We have to go with them. It's our only way off this ice island," he said to the old man.

"That thing looks like it will tip over if you sneeze."

"It's our only chance."

Reluctantly the old man followed Mokodihutt and the two Beothuk to the edge of the ice. The Beothuk pushed the tapaithook back into the water and held it for them to climb in.

"Don't step on the sides, just the very bottom where the rocks are, and then kneel there. You go there in the front," he said to the old man.

Mokodihutt interpreted for him.

Gingerly the old man put his leg over the side and slid to his knees on the floor with a hand firmly gripping each side. The two Beothuk grinned at each other.

"This the first time you've been in a tapaithook?" the younger one asked Mokodihutt.

Mokodihutt nodded and took his place in the middle between the two seats. He was kneeling on a sod that had been placed atop the flat rocks lining the bottom of the tapaithook.

The two Beothuk took their places and pushed off from the iceberg.

In a few moments, they navigated their way through the pack ice and reached the shore that had seemed impossibly far away to Mokodihutt and the old man when they were on the iceberg. With relief, they scrambled out of the boat onto the beach.

"Thank you," Mokodihutt said to his rescuers. "From both of us."

"Thank them for me," said the old man.

"I just did."

The Beothuk rekindled the fire they had left and warmed the meat from the feet of the monau. The skin was hanging in a nearby tree.

Mokodihutt and the old man devoured the meat that was offered to them and drank deeply from the water pouches. They sat as close to the fire as they could, letting the heat thaw their near frozen bodies. Neither of them had expected to see a fire again. Nothing else mattered now, just the warm food and the hot fire.

Mokodihutt and the old man followed their hosts along the coast a day and a half before heading inland. Much of the snow had melted away and the rivers and streams they crossed were swollen with rushing water from the run-off. The country was awakening in preparation for summer. Mokodihutt saw birds and animals he had never seen before. He watched the Beothuk pull sheets of thin white bark from some of the trees to feed the fire. The younger one explained it was also used to make their boats and containers for food and water and as covering for their mamateeks. Mokodihutt curiously ran his fingers over the smooth silky surface of the bark. It was unlike any he had touched before. He especially liked how the fire flared with a burst of heat when he tossed the bark on the flames. There was so much he was going to learn from these people. His excitement for the trip was returning; his ordeal on the ice quickly forgotten.

Once they turned inland they walked for another full day before reaching the Beothuk camp. The trails they followed were well travelled by both animals and man. Mokodihutt especially liked when the trail passed over a hill where he could get a view of the huge land with it's sparkling ponds, rolling bogs, and thick woods. This was a good place to live, he could tell.

He felt the old man was watching him and he glanced at him to find his face split by a wide grin.

"It's all so different. Better than I had even imagined," he said, matching the old man's grin.

The old man nodded, his eyes twinkling at the boy's excitement. Gone was the fear and panic he had seen in his eyes on the island of ice, now replaced with wonder and excitement at each new thing he saw. He shook his head at the mystery of youth.

Mokodihutt knew they were close to the camp when he saw the thin lines of smoke drifting over the trees. Shortly after, he heard the shouts and laughter of children in the distance. He quickened his pace a little, crowding the younger Beothuk on the trail ahead of him. When they stepped from the edge of the woods into the large clearing he came to a halt, taking in all the new sights. There were many mamateeks covered in the white bark just like the young one had told him. The bark had all been stained red. In fact, everything he saw had been stained red. There were Beothuk everywhere. It was the size of the village they had left in the frozen land. They stood around their fires and in front of the mamateeks staring at them as they approached. The clearing had become very quiet except for some of the younger children. They had bunched together and were pointing excitedly at the strangers dressed in furs.

"It's ok," said the older Beothuk. "We found them stranded on the ice. The younger one is Beothuk. The old S'kiemoo was taking care of him. They will cause us no harm."

Mokodihutt watched as a tall man wearing several feathers in his hair stepped out of the door of one of the mamateeks. Most of the Beothuks turned toward him to hear him speak. He must be the chief, thought Mokodihutt.

"Why have you brought them here?" he asked, addressing the older Beothuk standing next to Mokodihutt.

"We rescued them."

"The S'kiemoos are our enemies. You don't bring your enemies into your home."

"They are no danger to us. They needed our help. The boy spoke to us in our language."

"What's he saying?" the old man asked Mokodihutt.

"Just be quiet for now," whispered Mokodihutt.

The chief turned to Mokodihutt. "Who are you?"

"I am Mokodihutt, son of Kadimishuu and Ossaweet," he replied with a confidence in his voice that he didn't feel inside.

"Why are you dressed like that?"

"We live in the frozen land across the water. We have to dress in these heavy furs to protect us against the cold."

"Why are you with him?"

"This man is from the village where we live. He is my father's friend. He promised my father he would look out for me."

"You live with these people?"

"In the same village."

"Why?"

"We are the only Beothuk family in that area. They welcomed us into their village."

"How did you get here?"

Mokodihutt relayed the story to the chief as the rest of the villagers listened.

"You were very lucky."

Mokodihutt nodded nervously, waiting for him to continue.

"You may stay here with us, but you have to keep an eye on him. If anything happens he must go."

The chief turned and re-entered his mamateek.

Slowly the crowd returned to what they had been doing, while the children milled around Mokodihutt curiously, touching the fur skins he was wearing.

"What just happened?" asked the old man.

"He is the chief. He said we can stay."

The older Beothuk pointed to a mamateek set a little back from the others. "You can have that one," he said. "Someone will bring you food," he announced over his shoulder as he turned and walked away.

Chapter 16
1746

"They should have been back by now. Something has happened. I know it has. I can feel there's something wrong. What are we going to do Kadimishuu? I knew we shouldn't have let him go."

Ossaweet stood near the fire wringing her hands as a tear rolled down her face. Another tear followed the first, finding a new path down her lined cheek.

Kadimishuu looked at her sadly. He knew she was right. They had been gone too long, however the fact that none of them had returned gave him some hope. It would soon be winter. Maybe they had run into trouble and were going to hole up for the winter. It was the only thing he had to hang on to. He had to believe Mokodihutt was still alive.

He glanced across the room at his seven-year-old son who was curled up on his furs. Kassussabook was not strong like his brother. He had been sick for most of his life with one problem or another. This climate was not good for him. They should move away from here to give him a better chance, he thought.

"I believe he will return," he said with conviction. "They are all together and he is alright. Be patient Ossaweet. It might not be until after the freeze but they will be back."

He saw the glisten on her cheek and it tore at his heart. He wished he could do more.

The plan that he had been working on surfaced in his mind again, just as it always did when he had time to think. He had spent so much time thinking about it, he figured he had every detail covered by now. Soon he would have to tell Ossaweet. He was surprised she hadn't suspected something by now. This was a small community and it was hard to keep secrets around here.

He had worked out with one of his friends to trade for one of the wooden boats. It was his plan to take his family and sail to the island where his son had gone. He believed if he could get there he could find Mokodihutt. Also, it would be a better place for Kassussabook. He had been told the winters were not as harsh so it would give him a better chance at a good life.

He had not told Ossaweet because he did not want to get her hopes up until he was sure they could do this. He knew she would have wanted to leave right away if she thought she would find Mokodihutt, but he didn't think he was ready yet. It would be better to wait until after the freeze.

His friend had taken him out in the boat a few times lately and taught him how to sail, and he was getting comfortable with it but he hadn't done it on his own yet. That would be the final test for him.

The other thing he was worried about was finding the island once he left the village. His friend had been there before and did his best to describe where it was and how to get there, but most of it seemed to be intuition to Kadimishuu. He had shown him the stars to follow, but that only worked at night. This was his biggest concern and he spent much of his time fretting about it.

He knew he had to wait until the winter passed and the ice moved south, taking the storms with it. That would be the safest time and would put his family in the least danger. As anxious as he was to find Mokodihui it wouldn't be smart to take any chances on the crossing.

He hoped this was not just an old man's dream.

He decided he would tell Ossaweet after the freeze; besides, he still had to get some more furs for the trade.

The boats had been pulled out of the water and covered for the winter. They were just lumps of snow on the landscape now. The villagers still had not returned. Most everyone had now given up all hope of seeing them again; everyone except

Kadimishuu. He knew if he could get to the island after the melt he would find their son. Standing outside the newly constructed snow house, he gazed up into the night sky at the twinkling lights. He felt Mokodihutt was looking at those same lights somewhere out there. Their ancestors would guide them to each other soon. They just had to get through the winter. His hand involuntarily touched the scar left by the washawet. It was something he did whenever he was lost in thought. Most of the time he was unaware he was doing it.

He decided he would tell Ossaweet his plan tonight. It was time. He dropped to his knees in the snow and crawled inside.

As his eyes adjusted to the dim light, he saw Ossaweet watching him across the room. Kassussabook was already asleep underneath a pile of heavy furs. He was not a well boy. He slept a lot and seldom went outside. He sleeps too much, thought Kadimishuu.

"What have you been hiding, my husband?"

"Hiding?" he asked, temporarily taken off guard.

"Yes, hiding. You have not been yourself. At first, I thought it was because of Mokodihutt, but now I think it is more."

Realizing he had not been keeping the secret as well as he thought, he looked Ossaweet in the eye and smiled. "It's not so easy keeping something from you is it."

"No, it is not. Don't you think I know you, Kadimishuu?"

"I have a plan," he blurted out.

"A plan? What kind of plan?"

"We are going to find Mokodihutt."

Ossaweet sat there in silence looking at Kadimishuu incredulously.

"What are you talking about?" she finally said.

It all came spilling out in a rush. All the plans and details he had been keeping to himself for so long were now out there.

He watched her face as he talked and slowly a smile of excitement began to draw up the corners of her mouth. If it wasn't so dark, he thought he might have seen a twinkle in her eye.

"You have thought this out, haven't you?" she finally said when he stopped talking.

"I have."

"Do you really think we can do this?

"I do."

"Do you think we will find him?

"I do."

"I'm so happy, Kadimishuu," she said as she crawled across the floor and fell into his arms.

Every day, Kadimishuu watched the ice grow darker as it became thinner out in the bay, willing it to disappear. The snow was melting faster and some bare patches of ground were scattered around the village. Down near the beach, the boats were once again visible on their storage racks. The long harsh winter was behind them and both him and Ossaweet were anxious to get going. Even Kassussabook seemed a little excited, and he seldom got excited about anything.

They had everything ready. All that was left was for the ice to float out of the bay, to allow them to get the boat into the water. A few more days, thought Kadimishuu. He felt Ossaweet's arm slip around his waist as she stepped up to his side and laid her head on his shoulder.

"It won't be long now before we go find our boy," she murmured happily.

Everything had been loaded into the boat and checked at least twice by Kadimishuu. It was time to go. He felt a nervous tension as he hugged his friend. He was giving him last minute instructions, telling him once again the landmarks to look for on his journey. The tricky part would be recognizing when he reached the place where he had to leave the coast and make his way across the open water. He climbed into the boat, made his way to the middle seat, and shipped the oars. Over Ossaweet's shoulder, he watched the group standing and waving on the shore as he rowed out of the bay and around the point. He knew this was the last time he would see them. They would not return here. These people had been good to him and his family and he was going to miss them. He glanced behind him at Kassussabook who was huddled under several furs at the front of the boat. In his hand, he was clutching the whale carving one of the villagers had given him just before they pushed off from the shore. Despite the thick coverings, he looked cold. Kadimishuu smiled at him reassuringly and turned back to his rowing.

Once they cleared the point, Kadimishuu pulled the oars into the boat, lifted the small mast, set it in the hole through the seat, and unfurled the sail. The wind was light but strong enough to fill the sail and push them along. He moved to the back and sat next to Ossaweet where he could hold the sail rope and steer the little boat. He showed her how to hold the tiller and soon they were moving through the water at a much faster pace than when he was rowing.

Even though the sky was overcast with no sign of the sun, he was enjoying this. He could tell from the look on Ossaweet's face that she was feeling the same as him. Each part of the coast that slowly drifted by on the right was a sign that they were getting closer to Mokodihui. Soon their family would be complete again.

There was very little floating ice in the water, other than the occasional iceberg, so they didn't have to worry about hitting anything. It was turning out to be a more pleasant ride than he had expected. This sailing thing wasn't so hard. He wondered why he had been so nervous.

Kadimishuu picked up the bailing bucket and scooped up the water that was seeping through some of the seams and tossed it over the side. His friend had explained that it was normal to get some water coming in since the boat was lying up all winter. It needed to be in the water for a while for the boards to soak and expand, he had told him.

"It will be fine in a few hours," he reassured Ossaweet when he noticed her watching him anxiously. "All boats do this, especially first time in the water for the season. Why don't we have some lunch."

He sat back on the seat and took the dried meat she held out to him. Kassussabook was asleep under the furs in the front. They sat there in silence, watching the rugged coastline slip away behind them as they left their old life behind.

Kadimishuu noticed they were being pushed farther from the shore by the wind that was blowing off the land. He tried to adjust the sail to "tack against the waves" as his friend called it. He hadn't mastered that one yet and he wasn't making much progress now, but he wasn't concerned. If he could see land he would be alright, and if they got too far out he would drop the sail and row again. He knew they would still have coastline to follow until probably mid-afternoon and then they would have to cross open water to reach the island. That was how his friend had explained it.

"I'm thirsty," said a voice coming from the pile of furs in the front.

Ossaweet picked up one of the two water pouches and crawled to the front of the boat, keeping her head low as she passed under the sail.

Kassussabook's face emerged from the furs and he looked around him sleepily. "Are we there yet?" he said.

"No son. We have more sailing to do yet," Kadimishuu replied with a smile.

Kassussabook reached for the water pouch and took it from his mother, letting it slip through his fingers as the boat lurched a little in the water. Ossaweet grabbed it from the bottom of the boat before much of the water had spilled out and held it up to his lips. Kassussabook took a long drink as he watched a massive iceberg slide past far out on their left.

"What are those dark spots," he asked.

"Those are monau," his father replied.

"Do you think we will see one of these?" he asked, holding up the whale carving.

"Maybe."

"I don't want to. They are too big. They might tip over the boat."

"They don't bother with boats."

"I still don't want to see one. That would be scary."

Kadimishuu looked at the coastline. It was now blue. The wind was still blowing off the land and had pushed them farther out to sea. He could feel the wind on his face a little stronger and it seemed the boat was moving faster, splashing down on the waves that had grown larger.

He loosened the rope and let the wind bleed out of the sail and tried tacking again. It looked as if they had reached the end of the coastline and were at the point where he needed to steer the course for the island. In the distance, he could barely make out what looked like the high sheer cliff that his friend had told him to look for. He wished he had stayed closer to the shore. This was the part he had worried about the most. He needed to steer into the waves to get the boat closer to the land they were about to leave behind.

A sudden gust of wind filled the sail, yanking the rope from his hand. The small boom swung wildly across the boat, narrowly missing Ossaweet who was crawling back to where he was. She reached up and grabbed the boom as it passed over her head and held on. The boat wallowed and tipped dangerously on its side. Water spilled in over the edge and Ossaweet screamed as she tumbled against the ribs of the boat. The water pouch she was carrying flipped into the ocean and sank out of sight.

Kadimishuu managed to snag the sail rope and pulled it tight. The sail filled and pulled the boat upright again. Spray showered over them as the bow cut the waves. He tied off the rope and crawled to where Ossaweet was lying.

"Are you alright?"

"Yes, but I lost the water pouch."

"We have another one. That is plenty."

Kassussabook was crying, huddled down in the furs as far as he could get.

Kadimishuu began to bail the water out of the boat.

The boat was rocking more wildly as it rode to the top of each wave and splashed down into the next one. Most of them now had tiny white caps. The strong wind had suddenly come out of nowhere. There had been no warning. Anxiously he looked behind them. The land had disappeared in a wall of rain and wet snow that was sweeping down on them.

A numbing feeling of panic swept over him and he grabbed his knife and cut the sail free from the boom. It flapped wildly in the wind, adding to the noise and confusion. The boat wallowed in the waves that were now bigger than the boat itself. More water washed in over the sides. He was scared. He had not planned for this. This was more than he could handle. They were in big trouble. He had no idea what to do.

Ossaweet was on her knees bailing, desperately trying to keep ahead of the water that was coming in over the sides.

He had to get the mast out of the seat. It was too high and threatened to tip the boat over. Besides, he needed to sit there to row.

He braced his feet against the rocking sides of the boat, wrapped his arms around the sail-draped mast and pulled upward. Nothing moved at first until the boat lurched against a wave and it came free, crashing into the water and flinging Kadimishuu against the side of the boat. The blow made him lose his grip on the mast and it slipped away on the next wave. His right arm was pinned under him and, when he tried to move, a searing pain flashed up into his shoulder. He groaned in agony. Suddenly, a wave hit the boat and rolled him to the other side.

Ossaweet crawled to him and held him down. "What do we do?" she shouted in his face.

Kadimishuu stared into the terror-stricken face of his wife and was overwhelmed with the hopelessness of their situation. Using his left arm, he pushed to his knees and emptied his stomach. He had a sudden realization that he had killed them all.

The howling wind almost covered his son's cries. Ossaweet sobbed on the floor next to him. The boat rode high on the next wave and swooped down the other side, crashing into the water at the bottom, jarring his damaged arm. Water poured in over the front, soaking the furs covering Kassussabook. He began to wail uncontrollably.

Kadimishuu shook his head, trying to clear his thoughts. "We have to get the oars out and try and keep the boat straight," he said to Ossaweet.

"There's only one left."

He looked at her in despair. Behind her he saw the curling white froth of a large wave bearing down on them. He tried to wrap his good arm around her as the water came crashing over the tiny boat and pushed them down into the unforgiving arms of the cold dark water.

Chapter 17
1748

Mokodihutt sat in the near darkness, listening to the old man sleep. The fire had died to a soft glow, occasionally flaring, fanned by the draft that managed to find its way under the washawet skin door. The faint light was not enough to reach the sides of the mamateek, but it did reveal the shadowy figure of his friend huddled in thick furs, asleep on the other side of the fire.

Three years had passed at the Beothuk camp. Mokodihutt had been accepted into the band and was now an integral part of it. It had not been so easy for the old man. The band members had treated him with suspicion from the outset. There were some who did not want him there and openly pushed the chief to banish him.

"He is the enemy," they argued. "His people killed ours. He should not be allowed to live here among our people," they had said. Some thought he should be killed.

The old man had mostly kept to himself. Several times he had told Mokodihutt he feared for his life. It worried Mokodihutt a little.

Often during the long winter nights, alone in their mamateek, they talked about their home back in the frozen land. Even tonight before he went to sleep they'd had another conversation about it. They both missed their families and longed to see them again. The old man had only his wife waiting for him. They had had no children. Maybe that is why he wanted to look after me, Mokodihutt thought. He had grown fond of the old man and found himself leaning on him like a father.

"Do you think you could find your way home?" he had asked the old man one night.

"Perhaps, but it is a long way and we would need a real boat. Not one of those flimsy boats they use here. We would never be able to cross the water in that," was his reply.

"So, there's not much chance of that happening is there?"

"No, I don't think there is. You must make your home here now. This is a good place for you. You are with your people."

Mokodihutt remembered sitting in silence for a while mulling over what the old man had said. He knew his words were right. Although he missed his mother, father, and his little brother, and wished they could be here, he really didn't want to go back to live in the frozen land. He liked it much better here.

"But no one here wants you around," he had finally said.

"That will change in time. Have patience, boy."

It's been three years now and not much has changed for him, thought Mokodihutt.

He poked idly at the fire with a stick. His mind drifted back to his first caribou kill. After their first year at the camp he had settled into the pattern of life there. He joined the hunting parties. They taught him to hunt and soon he brought home his first caribou. He remembered how proud the old man had been of him and how they had celebrated together by eating its heart, here in the mamateek. It had been a special time for Mokodihutt and he was glad he had the old man to share it with. If he closed his eyes, he could hear the old man saying, "You are becoming a man, Mokodihutt." He smiled as he stared into the fire.

That had meant a lot to him then and still did. The old man was the only family Mokodihutt had.

Outside, the storm was building. Unobstructed by trees, it raced down the ice-covered lake toward them, tripping and rolling in on itself in its hurry to reach the tiny mamateeks lining the shore at the far end. He could feel it coming, rushing towards him.

He looked over at the dark form of the old man, huddled in his furs, asleep already, as if there was nothing going on outside. Mokodihutt smiled to himself.

Then the storm arrived.

It was like the winter storms he remembered from home. The only difference was that back home inside the snow house it had little effect, but in these mamateeks you could hear and feel the fierceness and anger of the storm. The winds howled and whipped the sides of the mamateek in their frenzy, hurling snow at it from every direction, determined to bury it if they couldn't knock it down. There was nothing to do but huddle in the warm furs and sleep just as the old man was doing. He placed some larger wood on the fire, pulled the furs a little tighter, and lay down.

When Mokodihutt woke early the next morning all was quiet. He looked up at the sloped ceiling of the mamateek. It was still standing. He pushed back the furs and looked across the smoldering fire for the old man. He was not there. With mounting alarm, he realized the old man's sleeping furs were gone. Why would he have taken those, he wondered.

He looked at the door where a small pile of snow had found its way inside. The lashing at the bottom was untied. With a sinking feeling, Mokodihutt untied the others and crawled out into the deep snow. There were no tracks to follow, just an unbroken sea of white. The storm had erased all signs.

He pushed his way to the nearest mamateek and crawled inside. "I need help," he said. "The old man is gone."

The three men inside looked at him thoughtfully.

"Why should we look for him?" asked the oldest. "He is not one of us. Let him go."

"He may be hurt. He is my friend."

"That may be, but he is not ours." He turned back to the fire in dismissal.

Mokodihutt pushed back out into the snow and made his way to the next mamateek.

There he managed to get two of the men to agree to search with him. He decided not to ask any further. He knew some in the camp still did not want the old man to be living there.

The three of them looked all day but found nothing. The old man had disappeared without a trace.

Mokodihutt spent his nights alone in their mamateek now. He missed the old man. He missed their conversations about the frozen land. He wondered what had happened for him to venture out into the storm. He knew the old man had never felt welcome here. Maybe he had decided it was a good time to leave, under the cover of the storm. He was no stranger to winter storms; he had spent his life around them. But why now? He had admitted that there was no way to get back to the frozen land, so where did he go?

Mokodihutt suspected he had wanted it to end. He hoped it had not been that way. Thinking of him still brought tears to his eyes.

When he had left so had Mokodihutt's last link to his family and his former home. Deep in his heart he knew he would never see them again. Sometimes he would sit and stare at the stars, the same stars that were over his home in the frozen land. His father had told him those flickering lights were the spirits of his ancestors. It was comforting to know they were watching over him.

He had been alone in this mamateek for almost a year now. The only thing that remained to remind him of the old man was one of his fur mittens that was hanging from the shelf overhead. He had become his family. The faces of his brother, father, and mother had faded, and his memories became less and less clear. That made him sad, but with time it became less and less painful.

He spent his time now with the other young men of the band, roaming the countryside, learning the ways of his people. He especially liked the nights around the campfires when the older people of the band told stories of their ancestors. Eventually they asked him to tell his story. The younger children especially liked the one about the great white washawet. It was one they asked for again and again.

Chapter 18
1753

Thoowidgee was born in the season when the trees were being consumed by inner flames. The forest was ablaze with the brilliant reds, oranges, and yellows that signaled the change in season. Soon would come the chilling winds, intent on erasing all color from the landscape, as they meticulously stripped the leaves from every branch and then covered the ground where they lay with a heavy blanket of white.

His first cry was not heard by his father. He had not yet returned from the coast. Mammashoot hoped her husband would come home soon. She wanted him to meet their son. She knew Mokodihutt would be excited that she had given them a boy. He had been impatiently waiting to find out since the day she had told him they were going to have a baby. In fact, she suspected that was some of the reason he had agreed to take this trip with some of the other men from the camp. He needed time to pass quicker; to be busy at something. The hunting party had been gone for almost two weeks and it was time for them to return.

The women who had been with her during the birth had gone home and she was alone in the mamateek with the baby.

She stared at his chubby little face in adoration while running her fingers lightly through his tangle of thick black hair. She could see Mokodihutt in his face, in the dark eyes that stared back at her. Her husband would like that, she thought as she smiled to herself.

She glanced at the ragged old fur mitten hanging from the ceiling. Mokodihutt would not get rid of it. He had told her the story of the old man so many times she felt she knew him, even though she had never met him. She would have liked to. Mokodihutt spoke so fondly of him. He would have made a great grandpa for this little one.

At times, she would get Mokodihutt to teach her words of the strange language he and the old man spoke. She was intrigued that Mokodihutt could speak another language, even though he never had occasion to use it anymore.

His stories of the old man's people fascinated her. They seemed so different from the Beothuk. She wanted to meet them someday, but that probably would never happen. They were the sworn enemies of the Beothuk and most of the camp feared them. That meant she couldn't talk about them around the camp, only to Mokodihutt in the privacy of their own mamateek.

Somewhere out there in the night, the lonely howl of a moisamadrook interrupted her thoughts. Frightened by the sound, the baby began to cry. She picked him up off the floor where she had laid him and held him close, gently rocking him back and forth as she walked around the small enclosure.

Mokodihutt had replaced all the birch coverings on the mamateek earlier in the year, so they would be well protected from the cold wind and snow when it arrived. This would be a happy winter, just the two of them with little Thoowidgee. It would be fun to watch him grow while they waited inside for the land to thaw. The thought made her feel a warmth deep in her chest and she hugged him a little tighter. She loved the wonderful new feelings this little baby was creating in her.

She began to sing softly to Thoowidgee. That was the name she had told the other women that she would convince Mokodihutt to give their son. As she passed underneath the mitten, she looked up and began to sing some of the words Mokodihutt had taught her. She smiled contentedly.

Then without warning, a searing pain erupted inside her head, filling the room with flashes of blinding light and just as quickly turning her world black. She slowly crumpled to the floor, spilling the baby from her arms as she fell.

Mokodihutt found her there the next day when he pulled back the caribou skin door and entered the mamateek. He had been told the baby had come by one of the women he met as he crossed the clearing. The news had quickened his step, and he was smiling broadly as he lifted his head as he stepped inside the mamateek.

"Mammashoot, I'm back," he said. "I hear you've got some good new..." The words froze in his mouth as he took in the scene before him.

His wife was lying on the ground close to the ashes of the cooking fire, crumpled in an unnaturally twisted position. He rushed to her side and knelt over her. Her skin felt cold to the touch. With a sinking feeling, he knew she was gone. A low moan escaped from his lips as he settled back on his heels. His eyes were blurry with tears as he looked around the mamateek, soon spotting the little bundle where it had rolled into the sleeping hole. One tiny little foot was sticking through the folds of cloth. Gently, he reached down, scooped it up, and held it tightly to his chest. Without the fire, it had become very cold inside the mamateek. He was afraid it was gone as well. Then it gave a weak whimper as Mokodihutt gazed into its tiny eyes. The sound wrapped around his chest and squeezed, making it harder to breathe.

He turned back to Mammashoot and sobbing he whispered, "Thank you, my wife. You have given me a beautiful baby. But what will I do now?"

He sat there on the floor for a long time, cradling the little one and quietly sobbing for Mammashoot. They had so many plans, so much they wanted to do together. Now it was all gone, forever.

Having cried his tears, he became curious as he sat in the stillness of the mamateek, rocking his little bundle. He unwrapped the cloth to check. "A boy," he exclaimed aloud. "You gave us a boy."

They had planned to have many children. This little one would be the only one. They had talked of someday moving to the Great Lake. Now he and his son would have to do it alone. In a moment, life had changed and could never be the same.

The baby began to whimper. Mokodihutt looked down into its watery eyes.

"You're probably hungry," he said. "I'd better find someone to help. I wonder what she planned to call you?"

He took the baby to the next mamateek where he found one of the new mothers who had helped Mammashoot. She turned as he entered and smiling said, "There's little Thoowidgee."

Her smile faded as she saw the streaks that the tears had left on Mokodihutt's face. "What's wrong?" she asked in alarm. "Is Thoowidgee alright? Where is Mammashoot?"

Mokodihutt nodded. "Is that the name she gave him?"

"Is something wrong with Mammashoot?"

He held out the baby to her. "She's gone."

"Gone? Gone where?"

"There was no life in her when I got there."

"I was with her last night. She was fine then. What could have happened?" she said with alarm.

"I don't know. She was just crumpled on the floor. There are no marks on her."

"Go to her," she said, holding out her arms for the baby. "I will take care of Thoowidgee. I can feed him."

Mokodihutt handed him over, then he turned and ducked out of the mamateek. He returned to their home and sat with Mammashoot.

Chapter 19
1763

Thoowidgee was ten. He loved when they moved to the coast each year, after the snow and ice had left the rivers. He liked the smell of the sea. It seemed as if the air was cleaner there than inland. He even liked the scent of the beaches at low tide. The rotting seaweed had a peculiar smell that never failed to trigger memories of past trips to the coast. He loved how big the sea was. There were always some little treasures it swept ashore for him to find each year. He could spend days roaming and searching for them.

He often wondered what was on the other side of all that water. He sometimes imagined someone like him sitting on a beach out there wondering the same thing.

Some days he just sat on the beach with his friend, Cattaawee, and Cattaawee's sister, Odensook, tossing small round beach rocks into the water, talking about what could be out there. Cattaawee thought nothing, but Cattaawee's sister thought the same as Thoowidgee. He knew there had to be more land out there. It didn't make sense that there wasn't. It was just too far away to see. He thought there were people out there too. Maybe like him, maybe not.

The three of them had been together ever since he could remember. Seldom could one be seen around the camp without the other two. Like Thoowidgee, Cattaawee was ten and his sister was just a year younger. Sometimes Thoowidgee wondered what it would be like to have a sister, but then he supposed he didn't need one of his own with Odensook around.

The band had built summer mamateeks at the mouth of a large bay. Each year it served as their base while they gathered monau, fish, and berries for the long winters back in the interior.

The bay was two days journey from the interior camp. Last night they had camped near a river. Just before dark, several caribou passed by the clearing following the heavily travelled path parallel to the river. A couple of men gave chase and took down one of them. There was fresh meat for the camp and they celebrated into the night.

Because of the late night, they got a late start and it was almost noon before they reached the place where the river ran into the sea. From here they would have to travel down the coast for almost another half day to reach the summer camp. Near the mouth of the river, a single mamateek was built back against the trees. There didn't seem to be anyone around, although the charred wood in the outside fire pit showed that it was lived in.

Mokodihutt, who was at the front of the group, pushed aside the door and bent to enter. He stopped immediately inside the door, causing the man following him to bump him from behind.

They stood there quietly surveying the scene before them. Two blood covered bodies lay on the ground near the centre fire pit. Back in the shadows a young girl sat with her knees drawn up and her back against the wall. Her long hair had fallen forward, covering her face. She pushed back her hair and looked up at the two men standing at the door. Her whole body was shaking and Mokodihutt could see the terror in her tear-filled eyes. Not registering that these men were her people, her eyes flickered around the mamateek like a cornered rabbit, looking for a way to escape.

"What happened here?" asked Mokodihutt softly.

He watched as the tension went out of her body on hearing her own language.

"They killed them," she sobbed.

"Who?"

"The Buggishamen. With their fire sticks."

"When?"

"Two days ago."

Mokodihutt dropped down on one knee in front of the young girl. She seemed to be about 16 or 17 years old. He could see the fear smoldering in her eyes.

"Who are they?" he asked gently, indicating the woman and young child on the floor.

"That's my mother and my little brother," she whimpered.

He turned to the man standing next to him. "Get one of the women to come in and take her out of here," he said quietly. Turning back to the young girl he said, "We will take care of your family. Where is your father?"

"He is buried back in the woods. He died before the snow left. They took my other brother," she continued. "He is nine years old. I don't know what they did with him."

"Where were you when this happened?"

"I was back in the woods gathering firewood when I heard the shots. I ran. They were leaving with my brother when I reached the clearing. I hid so they did not see me. There was nothing I could do, no way I could help him." She began to cry again.

"How many of them were there?"

"Two," she managed to get out between the sobs that were shaking her whole body.

"You go with her," he said as one of the women entered the mamateek. "She will take care of you. You are safe now."

He and the other man followed them out the door. By now the whole group had gathered outside the mamateek. Between them they told the others what had happened.

Immediately everyone started talking.

"Are we safe here?"

"No, we should go back. They may still be around."

"What about the boy?"

"We should follow them and take him back."

"We can't do that. They have fire sticks."

"We will all die."

"There are many of us and only two of them."

"They have fire sticks."

"We should go to our summer camp and then decide."

"Yes, we should do that."

Heads began to nod as the idea began to catch hold and soon it was agreed.

Before leaving, they buried the mother and baby inside the mamateek, covering their shallow grave with river stones.

The mood was much more subdued as they hurried along the coast. Men in front and at the back of the group watched the woods with hathemays drawn to protect the rest. There was little or no conversation. Everyone was filled with an expectation of danger, constantly scanning the woods around them.

It was late afternoon when they neared the summer place. The light was beginning to drain out of the day. The first sign of more trouble was the thick smoke billowing up through the trees in the distance.

The men hustled the women and children into the thicker woods where they wouldn't be seen. Then they cautiously made their way to the point that separated this cove from the one with the summer camp.

Standing at the edge of the woods, Thoowidgee watched them go. He looked at Cattaawee standing next to him and a slow grin spread across his face. Cattaawee nodded in agreement. Cattaawee was always up for an adventure and he wasn't about to miss out on this one. That was one of the things Thoowidgee liked best about his friend. They began to jog up the beach in pursuit of the men.

Ahead of them, the men had reached the neck of woods and had a view of the summer camp in the next cove. Thoowidgee watched as each of the men squat or kneeled behind the protective bushes and peered through. He could tell from their actions they were upset at what they saw.

As they got closer, Mokodihutt turned and held up a cautionary hand. The boys walked the rest of the way in a crouch until they were standing behind Mokodihutt.

Thoowidgee looked over his father's shoulder through the openings in the bushes at the darkening cove beyond to see what had upset the men so much.

The first thing he saw was the burning mamateeks. Standing around the blaze were several Buggishamen. He watched as one of them set the last mamateek afire with the torch he was holding in his hand. The sudden flare as the flame caught hold lit the scene as if it were the middle of the day.

Nearer the beach stood two partially built wooden houses that weren't there last summer. Two wooden boats floated in the quiet water of the cove.

On the beach near the water a large wooden rack stood on long poles. The top was covered with dry boughs.

"What is that?" asked Cattaawee.

"They use it to dry their fish," said one of the men. "I've seen it before. We will get lots of fish there tomorrow."

The men and boys stood there quietly watching as darkness fell. After the initial flash of the birch rind being consumed, the flames of the burning mamateeks died down to smoldering ruins. No one spoke. Each lost in their thoughts.

It wasn't the loss of the mamateeks that was so concerning as the loss of access to their summer camp. The Buggishaman had taken over the cove. Why this cove? wondered Mokodihutt. It was obvious his people were using it for a summer camp. Why would they destroy something that was not theirs?

"Go back everyone. We will camp in the woods tonight," he finally said.

They retreated along the beach to where the women were hidden. They had found a small clearing big enough to hold them all and had settled the children down to sleep. No fires were lit to alert the Buggishamen, and everyone was told to stay as quiet as they could.

Mokodihutt sat in the circle with the other men, their concerned faces barely visible in the faint light of the full moon. The conversation began.

"What should we do?"

"Kill them."

"Kill them? Why?"

"They can't steal our children, kill us, burn our houses, and not pay for it," said someone angrily.

There was a murmur of agreement around the circle.

"Is that the right thing to do?" someone asked.

"If we kill them, they can't do it again."

"Perhaps it will stop them from coming in their boats."

"What if that brings more of them? Maybe they will hunt us then."

"They want to take over our land. We need to stop them or we will have nothing left. If more of them come, we will deal with them."

Around the circle, heads nodded in agreement.

"How many did you count?"

"Five."

"We have nine men."

"We can surprise them from the woods. They won't be expecting us."

"They might."

"Did anyone see the boy?"

"No."

"They may have him inside one of those wooden houses."

"Should we sneak down there in the dark and find out."

"No. There is too much light. The moon is full. If we are seen we won't surprise them, and that is the only chance we have. If he is there we will find him tomorrow."

"We should do this just as they are waking up. They will be more confused."

"That way they won't get a chance to use their fire sticks."

"That's right. They must not get a chance to use those."

Thoowidgee and his friend Cattaawee sat just outside the circle listening to the men plan. He was both excited and scared at the same time, just like he knew his friend was. They had never been a part of something like this. They had heard stories of battles before but neither of them had expected to be this close to one.

His father turned around and looked at them. "You boys will stay at the edge of the woods and watch. If something goes wrong, you must return and lead the women and children away from here. If we find the boy we will send him to you."

Both boys nodded eagerly, happy that they were given something to do. Thoowidgee knew neither him nor his friend would get much sleep tonight.

Early the next morning, just a little before sunrise, the nine men and two boys assembled at the beach. Seven of the men were carrying hathemays and two were armed with their aaduths. All of them had long knives sheathed at their sides. The boys held their hathemays in their hands.

Thoowidgee rubbed his eyes. He was surprised he had fallen asleep. All he remembered was his father's hand on his shoulder shaking him awake. Suppose he had let me sleep and I had missed it, he thought with dismay. He looked at Cattaawee who was grinning at him, as if reading his mind.

He turned and followed the men as they quickly made their way along the beach to the point where they could look out over the cove where the Buggishamen were. There was no sign that any of them were awake.

They left the beach and quietly hurried through the woods until they were opposite the new wooden houses the Buggishamen were building. Smoke from the burned out mamateeks drifted over them, carried by the light wind. It served to remind them why this needed to be done.

The woods grew all the way to the edge of the beach, providing the cover they needed to surprise the Buggishamen. They hadn't cleared the trees yet, other than those they had cut for their houses. It was a short dash from the woods to the buildings. There was little risk they would be seen.

Mokodihutt took one last look at his son, turned, and ran with the rest of the men across the open ground to the houses. Four of them crouched against the wall of the first house and five against the second.

Holding his hathemay at arms length to keep it from hitting the wall, Mokodihutt pressed his ear against the side of the building. He could hear sleeping noises from inside. He motioned to the men at the other house to let them know there were Buggishamen inside. He waited for them to check their house.

He looked at the sky. Dawn was fast approaching. Already faint streaks of light had appeared over the horizon. In the nearby woods, birds were beginning to stir, chirping their morning songs. They needed to hurry before those inside awoke.

One of the men at the second house signalled there was no one there, so he motioned them back.

Keeping the rough boards of the wall against their backs, they slid around the corner to where three steps led up to the open doorway.

Three men crowded up the steps behind one another. The others gathered around the bottom step waiting for them to go through the door. The last step creaked loudly and someone shouted a warning inside as they all pushed through the opening. It was too small a space for their hathemays so they rushed the four sleepy Buggishamen with their knives drawn. More of the men rushed through the doorway to join those inside. One of the

Buggishaman managed to get off a shot, lighting up the small room with the flash, but it thudded harmlessly into the wall. Inside the crowded room the screaming and shouting was deafening.

The Buggishamen were overwhelmed and it was quickly over.

The men stood back, wiping their blades on the legs of their pants, surveying the scene.

"I thought there were five someone said."

Everyone in the room froze. The one nearest the door turned and stepped to the opening, raising his hathemay as he moved. The blast rocked the front of the house, tearing through his chest, throwing him backward on those behind him. Mokodihutt found himself flat on the floor underneath a tangle of arms and legs. His hathemay had snapped in two in the fall. He released it from his hand and pushed himself free in time to see the Buggishaman framed in the door opening with the fire stick pointed into the room.

It seemed as if time slowed down then. He could see every detail of his face; the ragged red beard, the bushy eyebrows with a thin scar running over one, the protruding nose centred between the two dark eyes, and the woolen cap pulled down to his ears. Another scar ran across his bare chest, markings of another battle he had survived. He had instantly taken in the scene in the room and was swinging the weapon toward the two men standing in the corner who had managed to grab their hathemays.

Mokodihutt watched the tension in his finger as he curled it around the trigger. He heard himself yelling a warning and then the Buggishaman jerked suddenly and grabbed at his back, pulling the fire stick upward where it blasted harmlessly into the open roof.

Still clutching at his back, he stumbled to his knees. Mokodihutt could now see the two arrows sticking out of his back. Those still on their feet rushed him with their knives.

Mokodihutt shook his head to try and stop the ringing in his ears. He looked up to see Thoowidgee and Cattaawee come through the open doorway. Their hathemays were at the ready with notched arrows.

His eyes met his sons and he nodded in acknowledgement. Thoowidgee had become a man today. He and Cattaawee had saved them. This story would be told around the campfire for many generations to come. He smiled as a surge of pride flowed through his chest.

They found the missing boy in the second house. His hands and feet had been tied together with the end of the rope lashed to a post. They set him free and told him where to find his sister.

The men had all gathered on the beach at the water's edge. Most of them had waded into the shallow water and were busy washing off the blood. The heat of the battle was still on them.

"We have to destroy all of this," someone said.

"Yes. Anything we can't use."

"Someone get those boats."

"Let's burn it all down."

"Leave nothing any more of them could use."

"Let's make sure they can't return to this place."

Several of the men went to work on the flake, pulling down the supporting poles until the whole structure collapsed in a heap on the rocky beach. Shortly after, the two boats grounded ashore and the men jumped out of them onto the beach. Together they pulled them out of the water and manhandled them unto the pile of logs and sticks that had been the flake. Using the dry boughs that had been spread over the top of the flake to hold the drying fish as kindling, the whole thing was soon ablaze.

They stood around watching the flames for awhile, letting the last of the battle adrenaline drain away as the initial heat forced them back a couple of steps. This time Thoowidgee and Cattaawee did not stand outside the circle. They were accepted as warriors for what they had done. Mokodihutt bent and pulled a flaming pole from the fire. "Burn the house," he said to Thoowidgee as he handed it to him. "The one where we found the boy. We have to take the heads of the Buggishamen in the other one before we burn it."

Thoowidgee took the flaming torch from his father's hand and he and Cattaawee broke into a run. After some coaxing they managed to get the structure alight, and stood back to watch their handiwork.

The others had done their work and had started a blaze in the second house. Soon the beach was covered in thick black smoke carried along by the light breeze.

They mounted the heads of the slain Buggishamen on long poles at the edge of the beach and left carrying their fallen comrade. Some of them carried bags filled with partially dried fish. They would not return here to this cove again.

"Why was that done?" Thoowidgee asked his father as they rounded the point to the next cove.

"What?"

"Their heads. Why remove their heads?"

"We release their spirits, son."

"But they are our enemies. Why do we care about their spirits?"

"They are men too, bad men, but still men. Just as you have been taught to respect the animals you kill, you must also respect other men, even those who would kill you. This way their spirits can't stay and roam the land. The Great Spirit will take care of them from here."

Farther up the beach they could see some of the band who had gathered to greet them. Thoowidgee and Cattaawee hurried ahead to find Odensook to tell her the story of their adventure.

Chapter 20
1769

Things had changed for Thoowidgee. This morning he and Odensook had gone hunting together without Cattaawee. Lately he had been noticing changes in Odensook. Something was different. She looked at him differently. There was something more behind those dark eyes he hadn't noticed before. It was stirring something deep inside him, something that was confusing him, yet it was a good feeling; a feeling he didn't want to stop.

He had seen her body before. The three of them had swum together since they were little. But today as she dropped her cloak and ran laughing into the warm water of the river it wasn't the same. Suddenly he had this overwhelming need to hold her close, to feel her warmth against him. At first, he was dismayed at the feelings that were coursing through him. She was his best friend. He hesitated there on the riverbank until her head came to the surface and she waved him in.

Leaving his clothes in a heap next to hers, he ran into the water and quickly closed the distance between them. As he approached her she playfully splashed water in his face and dove under the surface again. He followed, a new urgency driving him to catch her.

They surfaced, their faces inches from each other. She grabbed his head and kissed him full on the lips. After only a moment of surprise, he wrapped his arms around her and drew her tightly against him. Suddenly their worlds collapsed to the tiny space around them. Nothing else mattered. Nothing else existed.

Over the next few weeks Thoowidgee lost interest in everything except Odensook. The long summer nights were slowly growing colder, the forest changed to bright oranges and reds, yet Thoowidgee hardly noticed the changes. He had stepped into a world that he hoped would never end. He wanted those feelings to go on forever.

Cattaawee eventually gave up trying to get Thoowidgee to hunt with him and now mostly went alone. His best friend and his sister only seemed to want to be alone together in the woods. He was in the way and they didn't want him there. He decided to leave them to it. He figured they would get over it eventually and come to their senses. Then things would go back the way they always were, the way they should be. There wasn't much point hunting with Thoowidgee anyway. His head just wasn't in it.

And so it was that he found himself following a trail of caribou tracks on a chilly fall morning, almost a day's travel from the camp. A low-lying cloud of steam drifted over the bog as the early morning sun gently breathed its warmth on the frost covered grass. It seemed he was walking in the clouds as he followed the fresh trail. The other side of the bog was hidden by the mist that swirled around him as he passed.

He counted the tracks of at least five animals and he knew he would have one of them before the day was done. This would be a lot easier if Thoowidgee and Odensook were here, he thought, that is if they paid attention. With the three of them they could surround the caribou and pick the best one. Now he would have to take whatever animal was closest. It was more fun when the three of them hunted.

He tracked them out of the mist into the bordering woods. Just ahead he saw movement and he froze, letting his eyes adjust to the sunlight and shadows. At first he only spotted three grouped together in a stand of birch, but as his eyes searched through the surrounding trees, he found the other two, one to the left and one to the right. He slowly shrank to a crouch and pulled two arrows from the pouch at his side. He notched one and let the other dangle between the fingers of the hand that held the bow. He decided he would go for the one on the left. She was closer and there was more cover to allow him to get in range.

With no wind to take his scent away, he knew he would not get as close as he wanted. He began to crawl on his knees, keeping as low to the ground as he could. The caribou were grazing on the grass and small shoots at the base of the trees. They had no idea he was there.

He consciously forced his breathing to slow to relieve the tension he felt in the muscles of his back and arms. After what seemed a long time, he had managed to get as close to his target as he dared. He watched her graze for a moment, her head tossing as she pulled at the young shoots, stripping their remaining leaves with her teeth. He waited until she raised her head to chew. Marking the spot on her chest with his eyes, he drew the bow and released the two arrows in quick succession. He saw the first bite deep into her chest exactly where he wanted and the second hit close by. She reared back and snorted in surprise, startling the others who immediately raced away into the woods. Stumbling as her heart pumped its last, she tried to follow. Three steps were all she could muster before her head drooped and she collapsed.

He opened her, pulled out the steaming heart and sliced a small piece. As he chewed the bloody meat he thanked the Great Spirit for the kill. He wished Thoowidgee were here to share it with him. He wished he would get over his sister. He wanted the old times back.

Once he had removed the insides and the head, he slung the carcass over his shoulders and began the long walk back to camp. There will be fresh meat for the family tonight, he thought.

He reached the place he had camped last night just before the sun reached the middle of the cloud speckled sky. When he was halfway across the clearing he sensed he wasn't alone. Lifting his head from the awkward position it was forced into by the caribou on his shoulders, he looked directly into the eyes of a Buggishaman who was standing a couple of paces in front of him. Glancing to his right, he was surprised to see two more. They wore their trousers cut off at the knees with long stockings underneath. They had heavy woolen jackets and all three wore gray woolen hats over their long unruly hair. In their hands, they carried the long fire sticks.

Before he could drop the caribou from his shoulders, two of them rushed him and knocked him to the ground. One of them pinned him there with his knee grinding into his back.

Cattaawee could not move. It was a struggle to even breathe.

They bound his hands tightly behind his back and roughly pulled him to his feet. A short rope was tied to the binding around his hands. It was held tightly by one of the Buggishaman who used it to jerk him backward against a tree where he looped it around one of the larger branches.

Cattaawee looked around him wildly. He could feel blood trickling down his face from the scratches he'd gotten when he was thrown to the ground. They had taken his knife and his hathemay and arrows. He could see no way to escape from this.

The Buggishamen started a fire, cut slabs of meat from the dead caribou and roasted them. They were talking in a strange language that he could not understand. Occasionally they would look in his direction and erupt in laughter. Cattaawee was scared. The binding was cutting his wrists. His hands were going numb and his shoulders ached from the sharp angle they were pulled into. He thought about his sister and his best friend.

"Dat'll do nicely now won't it boys," said John, nodding at the Indian tied to the tree.

"Sure will," agreed Sam. "Skipper's gonna be some pleased wit us."

"Dat's fer sure."

"Don't drink all dat, Sam. Pass da bottle here, will ya," said Charlie.

"Tink he's one a da Indians dat raided our stage?"

"Probly."

"Looks young."

"Not too young fer dat."

"S'pose."

"What does it matter if he was one of 'em er not? He's Indian. Dat's all dat matters. Dey'd all steal da eyes right out a yer head."

"Das true," said Charlie, taking another long swig from the bottle before he passed it on to John. "Ya can't trust one of 'em, can ya boys?"

"Wat do ya tink da Skipper will do to 'im?

"Shoot 'im er hang 'im. Either way he's gonna die," laughed Sam.

"Gotta make an example of 'im, see."

"Dat'll teach 'em," chuckled John.

"How old do ya tink he is?"

"No more den 16 er 17 I'd say."

"Caribou is good."

"And he got it fer us."

"Saved us da trouble."

"Should toss 'im some, I s'pose."

"And how's he gonna eat it wit his hands tied behind his back."

"Oh, yeah. Never tought a dat. Oh well."

"Tink one of us should stay awake and watch 'im?"

"Maybe, but it ain't me. Too much ta drink."

"Me neider."

"He ain't goin' nowhere. Somebody toss some more wood on da fire."

"I wonder if dere's more of dem round here," said Charlie sleepily to his two snoring partners.

Cattaawee wriggled his hands in the bindings. There was no room to move. They had tied them too tight. He could feel the blood seeping down over his fingers. His arms ached, bringing tears to his eyes. His stomach growled at the scent of the cooking meat. He wondered what these Buggishamen were planning to do with him. He guessed they were not going to kill him or they would have done it by now.

He wished he had not hunted alone. He thought of his sister and Thoowidgee again. If they had been here this would not have happened. Perhaps they would come looking for him. He had been gone for two full days now, but then two days was not a long enough time for them to be concerned. It probably wasn't going to happen.

He leaned his head back against the trunk of the spruce tree and stared up through the thick branches The sky was dark enough to see all the twinkling lights of his ancestors.

"Help me," he whispered in despair.

He listened to the Buggishamen talking in their strange language at the fire. The words made no sense. He wondered what they were saying. He wondered where they had come from. Probably the land on the other side of the sea that Thoowidgee and Odensook were always talking about. Well if this is the kind of people over there, they had best stay there. There was no place for them here.

The Buggishamen were drinking something from the bottle they kept passing around. The more they drank the happier they seemed to get. Cattaawee wished he could have some to wet his parched throat and make him feel happy as well.

Before long they were all snoring around the dying fire.

Cattaawee watched them for a while until his eyelids finally grew heavy and he fell over on the ground and slept.

Charlie was the first to wake. Trying to ignore his pounding head, he crawled to the fire and rooted around the ashes until he found some live embers. He blew on them until they ignited and fed them with some dry sticks.

Glancing at the Indian, he saw he was still asleep and he pushed to his feet, shuffled to the bushes, and relieved himself of some of last night's drink. He drew in a deep breath of the crisp morning air, trying to get rid of the cobwebs wrapped around his brain. Behind him he heard the other two stirring.

"Marnin' boys."

"Cold one iddin't? Ya can see yur breath," said John as he scratched at his beard.

"Tis."

"Animals got at da caribou whiles we slept."

"Looks 'alf eaten."

"Some of it still good"

"Well at least no more Indians showed up. He's still there."

"I was tinkin'. It's only a lot a trouble to take him all da way back to da coast."

"How's dat?"

"We got ta be watchin' 'im all the time, even tho he's tied up he might run. Wha's da point?"

"What about da Skipper?"

"He won't care. Save 'im the trouble, don't ya tink?"

"S'pose it will."

"We could string 'im up and have done wit it."

"We got enough rope."

"Toss it over dat limb dere. It should be strong enough. Not much to 'im."

Cattaawee woke to the rough hands pulling him to his feet. His shoulders and back screamed with pain and he moaned softly. He couldn't feel his hands. Sleepily, he looked around him. He watched one of the Buggishamen throw a rope over the limb of a tall birch tree as the other two held his arms and led him toward it. He wondered what they were up to now.

As one of them slipped the loop in the end of the rope over his head he thought, this must be to keep me from running, but I will the first chance I get.

One of the Buggishamen holding him moved to the other end of the rope and grabbed it with his partner. Together they pulled the rope until Cattaawee's legs left the ground.

Cattaawee let out a silent scream of terror as the rope cut into his throat, closing his air passage. His legs began to flail wildly as he spun in circles trying desperately to find air for his starved lungs.

The Buggishamen tied the end of the rope to a tree and began to break camp.

Just before stepping into the woods behind his companions, Charlie looked back over his shoulder at the dangling Indian swinging in the light breeze. The weight of the hind quarter of caribou was already cutting into his shoulder. It was going to be a long day.

"Shouldn't he be back by now?" she asked. "It's been a long time. Cattaawee isn't usually away this long."

"How many days has it been?"

"Four. I'm worried."

"Do you want to go look for him, Odensook?"

"I think we should."

"Which way did he go?

"He said he was going downriver to hunt caribou."

"Alright. Let's go find him. I'll get my hathemay and some food."

"Good. I'll get mine too."

They met back at Mokodihutt's mamateek, told him where they were going, and set out following the river downstream.

They stopped at noon to eat lunch.

"Do you think he came this way?"

"Not sure. All we can do is follow the river for now and look for his campfire. He would have camped by the river the first night I think."

"I think so too. My brother always does everything the same. He seldom changes his ways."

"Don't worry. We'll find him."

"I know. I just wish we had gone with him. At least now when we find him we can hunt together the way it used to be."

"Pass me some more of that dried meat."

"Wish it was warmer. I'd go for a swim."

"I'd love to watch you do that."

"This?" she said as her cloak slipped to the ground at her feet."

"Come here," he said, reaching out his arms for her.

A while later they were on the trail again. Thoowidgee noticed she seemed more relaxed than she had been in the morning. She skipped along the path ahead of him, twirling a bright red leaf between her fingers.

He was happy. She was going to make a good wife. They would have many children together. He smiled as he watched her.

Ahead, Odensook rounded a corner in the path and let out a scream of agony. He raced to her side in alarm. In horror, he looked at what she had seen. A few strides away, Cattaawee swung from the end of a rope that was looped over the limb of a tree. The birds had gone to work on his swollen face and he was barely recognizable.

"Stay here," he shouted at Odensook who had slumped to the ground. Drawing his knife, he ran to the tree. He sawed through the rope and Cattaawee fell to the ground with a sickening thud.

Odensook was sitting on the ground wailing.

"Who would have done this?" Thoowidgee wondered aloud in astonishment. He returned to Odensook and held her while she cried. His tears mingled with hers.

Eventually it dawned on him that whoever had done this to Cattaawee might still be around. He released Odensook and looked around at the woods that encircled them. He picked up his hathemay from where he had dropped it and notched an arrow. With one knee on the ground, he studied the woods carefully. He listened for signs of danger, but the only sounds were the crows scolding noisily from their perch atop the trees and the heart-rending sobs coming from behind him.

He pushed to his feet and walked to the burnt-out campfire. Next to it lay the partially eaten remains of a caribou. He kicked the ashes of the fire and a bottle went spinning away. He picked it up and looked at it. He lifted it to his nose and sniffed. The pungent smell made his nose wrinkle. Buggishaman, he thought. Only they would have a bottle like this. They did this to Cattaawee.

He returned to Odensook, knelt on the ground, and wrapped his arms around her trembling shoulders.

"Who would do such a thing Thoowidgee?" she sobbed. "That was so cruel."

"I think it was the Buggishaman. I found one of their bottles in the ashes."

"But why? What could Cattaawee have done to them?"

"I don't expect he did anything. You've heard the stories. They don't need a reason," he said angrily.

"He must have suffered so much. Oh Thoowidgee, why weren't we there to help him?

"You can't blame yourself for this, Odensook. No one could have seen this coming."

"I know."

They were silent for a while. Then Thoowidgee said, "We should bury him here."

"Why here?"

"We have no way to bring him home."

"Alright, but not beneath that tree. Beneath that one," she said, pointing to a large fir tree on the other side of the clearing.

Thoowidgee walked to the tree, dropped to his knees, and began scooping away the sod with his knife. Odensook joined him there.

Together they dragged Cattaawee's rigid body and placed him in the shallow hole between the large tree roots. They spent most of the remaining daylight covering him with stones from a nearby river.

Afterward, they lay down in each other's arms near the fresh grave and slept, all three of them together for the last time.

Chapter 21
1773

Thoowidgee looked around the crowded mamateek, the only home he had ever known. His father had moved into the mamateek long before he was born, and now it was clear they had outgrown it. It had been repaired and the wall coverings replaced numerous times but the original frame still stood. The wooden poles were smooth and worn bare of bark from the touch of his and his father's hands over the years. In some places notches were carved into the wood where he had idled away his time during the long winter days. His father had kept them all.

It held many memories, some good and some not. He had been born here and lost his mother here. A mother he had never gotten a chance to know. He had grown up in this place with his father as his guide. He had taught him how to hunt and how to survive the long cold winters. He showed him how to make a hathemay and the best young trees to use for arrows. He had taught him to treat the animals and his fellow tribe members with respect.

At his father's side, he had listened to the stories of his grandparents and his great grandparents. He could close his eyes and picture every memory to the very last detail. His father had patiently answered his questions and showed him the lights in the night sky that were his long-gone ancestors.

Together they had explored the country, but they never found a place they would have rather lived than here in this mamateek. They always returned to it.

Just a few years back it had become a home for his childhood friend and new bride Odensook. The mamateek had become happier and busier then. It was the first woman's touch the old structure had known since he was born. Things were soon re-organized around the mamateek, but his father had been good about it and let her make the place her own. Since then the mamateek had seen two girls birthed there and now their little brother Nonosabasut had arrived.

Thoowidgee looked at his father, who was smiling down at the squirming little bundle gently cradled in his arms. The deep lines that time had carved in his face seemed to run toward his wide mouth when he smiled, as if that was the way they were meant to be. His father had always smiled a lot, but it seemed it never left his face after his grandson was born. It was as if becoming Nonosabasut's grandfather had opened a new life for him; as if he had started over somehow. He loved to watch them interact. No matter what he was doing, his eyes were inevitably drawn to the little boy sporting the head of thick black hair.

Everyone else had to wait their turn to hold the baby if he was there.

He had begun to make him his first hathemay days after he was born and he sat with him for hours telling him the stories of his family, repeating them over and over again. "You have to remember all these things, little one," he would say. "Someday you will tell your grandchildren."

His eyes were not working the way they should and he no longer joined Thoowidgee on his hunting trips. He thought he would only be in the way. Because of this, he spent most of his time at camp. He had soon become the favorite of the camp children and fell quickly into the role of teacher. Seldom was he seen without a group of small children following him around the clearing or seated on the ground listening to his stories. You didn't have to watch him too long to see his love for children, and their love of being around him. They loved his antics, and the lively way he acted out his stories.

"It gives me something to do," he often said to Thoowidgee. "Makes me feel useful, not a burden. At least I'm doing something for the camp."

"It's time to build a new mamateek, a bigger one," he announced.

Odensook looked up from the cookpot and smiled knowingly at him. She knew what was coming next. She put her head down and kept stirring.

"This one is fine," came the reply from Mokodihutt without lifting his eyes from his giggling grandson's face, who had wrapped his tiny fingers around his grandfather's thumb and was pulling with all his might.

"It's not big enough, Father. We need more room. The family is growing."

"Plenty of room here."

"There are six of us now. There is not enough room to get around, barely enough room to sleep."

"Three of them are babies."

"Won't be long before they grow. Soon Nonosabasut will be crawling and we'll have three of them running around here."

Mokodihutt looked up at his son. There was a faraway look in his clouded eyes. "You know I can't leave here, Son. This is where I lost your mother. This is where you were born, where you grew up." He glanced up at the ragged bits of the mitten. "I lost my friend from the frozen land here." As in a daze, he said something in that strange language, and then his eyes returned to his grandson. The smile returned to his face.

"I am going to build it right next to this one. We can leave this one as it is," Thoowidgee pushed ahead, glancing at Odensook's bowed head for support.

"I won't be leaving. This is my home, and this is where I'll stay."

"Not even for your grandson?"

Mokodihutt didn't reply.

"I'm starting tomorrow," he announced.

Odensook was still stirring and smiling to herself.

Before a week had passed the mamateek was completed and they had moved in, all except Mokodihutt. Although he spent most of his waking hours in the new mamateek, because that was where Nonosabasut was, at night he always returned to his own to sleep, as he said he would.

Sometimes late at night Thoowidgee could hear him over there talking to his mother as if she were there in the room with him. He had only known his mother a few short hours, and he had been too young to have any memories of her. He didn't even know what she looked like, although his father often told him she looked just like him. All he had were the stories his father had told him about her. It was easy to see how much he missed her. He talked about her so much. Thoowidgee always wished he had been able to spend more time with her. It sounded like she would have been a good mother, perhaps like Odensook.

For some time now, Thoowidgee noticed the stories were changing. At first, he thought his father was changing them to make it more interesting for the children, but then he seemed to be leaving out things, as if he had forgotten them.

Then came the day when he entered his father's mamateek and found him staring blankly at the wet sharpening stone in his hand. An aaduth was lying on the ground close to his knees as if he might have already used the stone on it.

"What's this for Thoowidgee?" he asked, holding up the stone.

"To sharpen the aaduth."

"Strange. I can't seem to remember how. Where is your mother? I haven't seen her all day."

"She's gone, Father," he said, looking at him curiously.

"Gone? Where is she gone?"

"She died, Father," he said gently. "Many years ago. The day I was born, in fact. Don't you remember?"

Tears welled up in his eyes and trickled down the lines of his face. "Why didn't someone tell me?"

Standing there, Thoowidgee's thoughts went back to the day two of the band members had found Mokodihutt at the bottom of a small cliff. At first, they thought he was dead. He wasn't moving and his head was caked in blood where he had hit the rocks that were scattered on the ground at the base of the rock face. When they reached him, they discovered he was breathing and brought him back to the camp. In a few hours he had revived, and in a day, he was back on his feet, but he had not been the same since. His memory seemed to be leaving him, a little at a time. The encounter today was the worst Thoowidgee had seen. Never had he forgotten something so simple, or something so important to him.

Thoowidgee blamed the fall on his father's failing eyesight. The way he described it, he couldn't see more than shapes, like people at a distance in a thick fog. He shouldn't have been wandering out in the woods alone. He needed to be watched more closely. He always told him to stay at camp, but sometimes he just wouldn't listen. He had to do it his way. He supposed he would feel the same in his shoes.

"What happened to her? She was here yesterday," Mokodihutt interrupted his thoughts.

"No, Father. She has been gone since I was born."

"She was here yesterday."

"No Father, she wasn't."

"You're confusing me, Thoowidgee," he said, shaking his head vigorously. "I saw her yesterday. I know I did, don't tell me I didn't."

"Put down the stone and come see Nonosabasut."

His face lit up at the mention of his grandson's name and he nodded eagerly.

He let the stone slip from his hand, pushed to his feet, and followed Thoowidgee from the mamateek.

On entering the new mamateek, he held out his hands to Odensook who was holding little Nonosabasut. She surrendered him up and off he went to sit by the fire, launching into one of his stories as he went.

"I think I'm going to have to sleep over there," Thoowidgee said quietly to Odensook, sniffing appreciatively at the bubbling pot on the cooking fire.

"Why? Is he getting bad?"

"Yes. I'm afraid he is going to wander off and hurt himself again. It could be worse next time."

"Things are getting worse every day, aren't they?"

"They are. I think eventually he is not going to know who we are. Today when I got there he was sitting and staring at the sharpening stone in his hand. He had no idea what it was for. And then he started asking for Mother. Says she was there yesterday."

"What are we going to do if he no longer knows us?"

"We must honor his wishes."

Odensook met her husband's tortured eyes. She knew Mokodihutt had made Thoowidgee promise he would not let him get to the point where he didn't know his family. She could see the battle that was happening inside her husband as the time seemed to be inevitably drawing ever closer. She knew he was torn between honoring his father's wish and the fear of having to carry it out.

"You could get someone else," she said.

"No. You know that is not our custom."

"It has been done that way before. It would be easier for both of you."

"It has to be me, Odensook." His eyes were drawn to the fire where his father was playing with Nonosabasut. It was such a happy scene. His chest grew tight and he swallowed loudly.

"He probably won't even know it is you by then," she said softly, following his gaze.

"That might make it easier. It won't be him. He will have already gone away."

She reached up and tenderly brushed away a tear that had escaped from his eye and trickled halfway down his cheek. "Have some food," she said. "It is not today."

Chapter 22
1775

The vivid but troubling memories of his last time with his father had invaded his sleep for almost a year. No matter what actions or suggested remedies he tried, he could not seem to make the dreams stop. The lingering images always left him with a sad and heavy heart that now seemed to be with him all the time. He had never expected his father's life to end that way and it had changed his life forever.

Odensook was worried about him. Even the news that they were having another baby hadn't seemed to help distract him. His happiness was gone and all that was left now was despair. Sometimes she wondered if it had been the right thing, to have carried out his father's wishes. It seemed to have had such a deep impact on her husband, much worse than she had ever expected. But it was done. There was no way to go back and change things. They just had to find a way for him to move past it. It was up to her to help him do that.

Two days ago, when she mentioned to him that he was talking and crying in his sleep, he immediately decided to spend the nights in the old mamateek to avoid keeping up the rest of the family. That's the way her husband was. Bad as things were for him, he still cared for the rest of them.

That had only lasted two nights. It turned out that sleeping there was too strong a reminder, as she had expected.

On the morning of the second day he returned to their mamateek and announced that he had made up his mind and he was going to tear the old mamateek down. She listened patiently as he talked through his decision. It's more to convince himself than me, she thought.

"I'm going to do it, Odensook, I must. I can't sleep there. It just makes my nightmares worse. Having that mamateek there is a constant reminder of that last day. That place should only have good memories, but they are all gone because of that one night. It was where Father wanted to stay, and that's where we had our last moments together, but I can't keep remembering him that way. I can't live like this anymore."

"I know, my husband," she whispered gently.

"I would burn it down, but it is too close to this mamateek."

Odensook had told him the baby would come this week. He would tear it down then. Maybe it would mark a new beginning. He hoped it might. He felt better that he had made the decision; now it was just a matter of getting it done. He had already put it off ever since he'd had the conversation with Odensook. He knew there was danger in that.

He looked up at the pole from which the tattered mitten had hung all his life. He had buried what was left of it with his father. It was his last connection with his former home in the frozen land. He knew his father would have wanted it that way. Maybe now he had finally reconnected with his old friend.

His eyes were drawn to the shallow bed that had been hollowed out in the floor. That was where his father had fallen asleep that last night. He looked down at his hands, almost expecting to see them shaking, just as they had that night as they gripped the long knife. That too was buried with his father.

He looked up through the smoke-hole at the blue jay perched atop one of the poles. Their eyes met for a moment and then it screeched its piercing cry and launched into flight.

Listening quietly, he noticed for the first time in a long time the noises outside the lonely mamateek; the wind gently rustling the early spring leaves, the rattling of the little brook flowing by the back of the mamateek, the excited cries of the children at play, and the quiet murmurs of the women attending his wife next door in their mamateek. He had resolved in his heart that he had to rid himself of this sadness and move on. He just wasn't sure what it would take to climb out of the hole he had fallen into. He hoped that destroying the mamateek would be it. There wasn't much more he could try.

The quiet was shattered by the first cry of the baby as it entered his world. He wondered what kind of world it would be, as he took a deep breath, pushed to his feet, and walked out the door for the last time. This time he did not glance back as he let the door covering fall back into place.

He held out his arms as one of the women stepped through the door of his mamateek with the noisy little bundle.

Holding the tiny wriggling boy at arms length, he smiled as he looked into his own eyes and said, "Welcome to this world, my son. You shall be called Kirradittii."

His daughters eagerly ran over, trailed by Nonosabasut. "Let me see him," they exclaimed excitedly, elbowing each other to get closer. Thoowidgee dropped to his knees and cradled him for them to see. Curious little fingers reached out to touch his face and tiny hands. Thoowidgee realized he was smiling as he watched his family. I haven't done much of that lately, he thought. He needed to do better, to be better for his family. This was all he had left now. Without family, he was nothing.

Chapter 23
1784

He rubbed his hands together to warm them, then slipped his fur mitts back on and kept opening and closing his fingers inside them. It was freezing out. He had been sitting in the snow for too long and the cold was creeping through the caribou skins he was wearing. He didn't know how much longer he was going to be able to do this.

He didn't like this sentry job, out here in front all alone. But he did have a good spot here on top of this small hill. He was well hidden behind a clump of short trees and he had a good view all around him. If there was any danger from the Buggishamen he would see it coming first and could signal the others. He knew they were counting on him and he needed to stay alert. He wished it wasn't so cold.

Nonosabasut had picked the spot for him. He had a good eye for that; probably why he was always picked to lead them into battle. His older brother had that way about him. He seemed to be a natural leader.

A light snow began to fall. Kirradittii pulled his hood tighter around his face and tried not to move any more than necessary. The snow would cover his hood and make him invisible to the enemy. He carefully scanned the woods again. Behind him he could see the first mound of snow where Nonosabasut and one of his friends were hiding. Farther back were other mounds where they had stashed extra ammunition to use in their retreat.

He turned back to look out over the valley again and his breath caught as he spotted movement. He squinted against the falling snow. As his eyes adjusted, he saw the dark figures creeping through the woods, keeping cover behind the larger trees. He counted six, no, there was another, and another. There were eight or nine of them, maybe more. He narrowed his eyes and concentrated on the movement to try and get a better count. They were way outnumbered. That was obvious. This was going to be trouble. Maybe they should just run. It was probably their only chance of escape.

He pushed himself down flat in the snow trying to make himself invisible. They were getting too close. It was time to go. Time to warn the others. He rolled and pushed himself to a crouched position, preparing to sneak back down the hill, when suddenly he caught movement on his left. One of them was there on the hill. He hadn't seen him coming. Without looking at his enemy, he bolted for the safety of his friends. The first shot whipped past his ear, slamming into the low branches of the tree he was passing under and dislodging a shower of snow that drifted over him as he ran down the hill. He could hear the war cries of his pursuer. His enemy sensed victory, Kirradittii could hear it in his voice. He ran faster, glancing at his brother as he raced past their hiding place. He dove behind the next mound of snow and turned to watch as Nonosabasut and his friend jumped the Buggishaman as he ran past. They quickly and easily overpowered him, taking him out of the fight.

The other Buggishamen had rounded the hill, and seeing their comrade in trouble, raced toward the two Beothuk, firing as they came.

"Hurry," Kirradittii shouted frantically to his brother as he saw some of the Buggishamen's shots hitting the snow around their feet. "Run."

Nonosabasut turned and ran as he saw his friend stumble and fall from a direct hit to the face. Weaving back and forth to confuse their aim, he made it to where Kirradittii was crouched behind the snowbank and he dove into its shelter.

Grinning at his brother, Kirradittii reached into their stash of ammunition and handed him two perfectly rounded snowballs and then selected two for himself. They looked at each other, and with a yell, jumped to their feet and pelted the three closest enemy. Before they could turn and run for the next defensive position, four more of them came crashing over the top of the snowbank armed with their own snowballs, and in moments it was over.

"That was a good one," laughed Nonosabasut as he untangled himself from the two that had tackled him. "Let's go get something to eat."

He waved to his father who had been watching the whole thing from his vantage point atop another small hill. He knew the three of them would talk about this one over the evening meal. His stomach growled with the thought.

Chapter 24
1793

It was spring. The rushing waters of the swollen rivers had mostly run off. The flooded banks were drying out and the trees had once again clothed themselves with leaves. There was a comforting warmth to the wind. New life was everywhere.

Nonosabasut and Kirradittii had travelled downriver with their parents and two sisters to their summer camp, leaving the warm winter clothing behind.

The site of the summer camp was now very familiar to them, having made the same trek for the last five years. It was about a half day's walk from the coastline, set on the slope of a gentle hill that separated the river from a large pond. There were two mamateeks there and they were joined by another family of four, a young mother and father and their two little boys.

They had arrived two days ago. The repairs had been made to the mamateeks and wood had been gathered for the fires. Nonosabasut and Kirradittii were anxious to get to the coastline to test their hunting skills. They hoped to try their new aaduth they had each worked on throughout the winter. All they needed was some unsuspecting monau.

Underneath a cloudless sky, they left camp next morning for the short hike to the coast. They were both in a good mood as Nonosabasut led them down the familiar trail at a fast trot. Like everything, it soon became a contest to see who would have to stop running first. This time it was Nonosabasut who broke from the run and knelt at the riverside to take a long drink of cool water.

"I could have kept going all morning," laughed Kirradittii. "You are getting old brother."

Nonosabasut lifted his face from the water and grinned at his brother. "Then why are you breathing so hard?"

"Doesn't matter. I beat you."

"Think there will still be monau at the coast?"

"If there's any ice left in the bay."

Nonosabasut pushed himself up from where he had been drinking. "Guess we'd better get out there to find out."

"Guess so. I'll take the lead this time."

A short time later he pushed through the low brush and stepped out onto the rocky beach to find the bay filled with floating ice pans. Dotting the gently rocking ice were many monau basking in the early morning sun. Before the animals even noticed their presence both brothers had taken out one each with their new aaduth.

"That was easy," said Kirradittii as they dragged the two monau over the rocky beach to the treeline. "Do you want to head back to summer camp or should we find a place near here to camp for the night?"

"There's no rush. Let's wait 'til tomorrow," Nonosabasut replied as he drew his knife down the length of the monau's belly, allowing the warm steaming insides to spill out onto the ground. "We passed a good spot just before we reached the coast. We'll stay there."

Kirradittii nodded as he bent over the contents of his monau and picked out the heart and liver, discarding the rest of the insides for the scavengers.

They awoke to driving rain and a dark angry sky. Everything was soaked. Nonosabasut stood to his feet and brushed against the branches they had spread over their heads last night, sending a fresh shower of water over Kirradittii and the warm coals he had been blowing on.

"Did you have to do that?" he muttered angrily. "How am I supposed to get the fire started with you dousing it?"

"Let's just go," said Nonosabasut as the sky was suddenly lit with a bright flash of light followed by thunder crashing and rumbling away in the distance.

"Let's. This is just a waste of time anyway."

They hoisted their monau onto their shoulders and trudged up the path toward camp with heads bowed and eyes squinted against the chilly driving rain.

As the morning dragged by, Nonosabasut increased his lead on his brother, and by the time he walked into camp he was well ahead and almost too far away to hear.

Kirradittii was surprised to see his brother drop the monau, pull his hathemay from his shoulder and break into a run. With mounting concern, he quickly did the same, notching an arrow as he raced up the gentle slope.

By the time he reached the clearing, he was breathing hard. Nonosabasut was kneeling over the still body of their father. Others were strewn around near the mamateeks.

Kirradittii looked around at the devastation in shock.

"What happened here?" he said breathlessly.

"They're all dead."

"All of them?"

"Yes. All of them," Nonosabasut spat the words.

Kirradittii sank to the ground and held his head in his hands. "No," he moaned as he rocked back and forth in agony.

Nonosabasut left their father's side to kneel by his brother. He wrapped his arms around him. Together they cried.

"Our youngest sister is not here," said Nonosabasut finally. "Tamarraa is the only one missing."

"Where is she?"

"I don't know. Maybe they took her."

"Who?"

"Them." Nonosabasut pointed to the body lying against the side of their mamateek. Kirradittii could see the hilt of a knife sticking out of his chest. "It's one of the Indians from the other coast. Father must have put up a good fight. At least he got one of them."

Kirradittii walked over to the fallen Indian, studied him for a moment, and then kicked him in the face, repeatedly. Nonosabasut grabbed his arm and pulled him away.

"What do we do now, Nonosabasut?"

"Go after her and get her back."

Kirradittii looked at his older brother. He could see the seething anger on his face. Slowly, he nodded yes. A coldness seemed to wash over him as the need to avenge his family welled up inside.

"First we must move the bodies inside the mamateeks. We don't have time to bury them now. We must go after Tamarraa. She is the only family left."

"When do you think this happened?"

"Probably late yesterday."

"Then they haven't gone far. We should be able to catch them."

They carried the limp bodies of the two boys and laid them on the ground next to their parents inside their mamateek.

Their mother and older sister had died inside their mamateek. Gently, they lifted their father and carried him inside. They wrapped the three of them in blankets and laid them in their sleeping holes.

Kirradittii wiped the tears from his eyes. "How many arrows do you have?"

"Seven."

"I have five."

"Take whatever weapons you can find in the other mamateek. I will take father's arrows."

Kirradittii returned in a few minutes with five more arrows and his aaduth.

"That should be good," said Nonosabasut.

They looked into each other's eyes for a moment, locked in a quiet embrace, and then stepped outside into the rain.

"How many of them are there?" asked Kirradittii.

"Not sure. I'd guess four from the footprints. They left that way. No more pretend battles, brother. This one is for real."

Kirradittii nodded. "Let's go," he said.

Nonosabasut led at a slow ground consuming trot. The trail was obvious even after all the rain. They didn't seem to make any effort to cover their tracks. I guess they don't expect anyone to follow, thought Nonosabasut.

He settled into a comfortable run that would quickly narrow the distance between them.

A short time later they reached the place where the group had camped for the night. Nonosabasut examined it carefully. The signs seemed to confirm that there were only four of them, and he found smaller footprints that he thought must be Tamarraa's.

It seemed they had not broken camp early, probably because of the rain. "They can't be too far ahead," he said quietly. "We will catch them soon. Are you ready for this, little brother?"

"I am."

Nonosabasut looked at the sky in the direction they were heading. It looked like the rain was easing up. He wanted to catch them before that happened, if he could. He started to run again. Behind him he could barely hear his brother. He had learned to run quietly in all those pretend battles they had. He was proud of Kirradittii. He wondered how this was going to turn out. There was always danger in going into battle. At least they had the element of surprise, and that might be enough. It had better be, because they were outnumbered. This had to happen fast.

The tracks were getting fresher so he began to slow down. The rain had stopped. He glanced up at the sky to see the scuttling clouds thinning out. Rain would have been better, he thought.

Soon he was down to a fast walk with his hathemay in his hand and an arrow notched in its string. Close at his side, Kirradittii carried the aaduth in his right hand and his hathemay in the other.

Through the trees, they caught glimpses of water of what appeared to be a large lake. In the distance, they could hear shouts; strange words they could not understand. Some of the shouts were higher pitched. A girl, thought Nonosabasut, probably Tamarraa. They slowed to a crouched walk, carefully watching the path ahead and the woods around them.

The trail took a sharp turn toward the lake just ahead of them. They approached it cautiously and peered through the protective screen of trees. The group was gathered down near the water's edge. The front of a tapaithook was drawn up on the grass with the back of it sitting in the water. It appeared they were preparing to leave in it.

Tamarraa was resisting the efforts of two of them who were holding her arms, trying to force her into the tapaithook. The other two were watching them with their backs to Nonosabasut. They were laughing at their two companions' struggle to get the girl into the tapaithook. They were all distracted and Nonosabasut knew they would never have a better chance.

They had open clearing to cross, but it was now or never.

He met Kirradittii's eyes and nodded. Together they broke from cover and began to run. He veered right and Kirradittii veered left. They made it halfway across before one of the men at the tapaithook saw them and yelled a warning. Nonosabasut and Kirradittii came to a stop. Nonosabasut launched two arrows in quick succession and Kirradittii threw the aaduth. Both men who had been standing with their backs to them went down and did not move again.

Tamarraa had spotted her brothers, and when the other two men released her arms in their haste to grab their weapons, she bolted toward Nonosabasut. Running directly toward him, she blocked his sight of her captors and he couldn't fire. One of the Indians at the tapaithook did, and Nonosabasut watched in dismay as the tip of the arrow suddenly appeared in the front of Tamarraa's chest. With a look of curious surprise on her face she clutched at it, stumbled, and fell. Lying face down on the ground, she managed to raise her head enough to meet his eyes and she feebly stretched out her hand toward him as her body shuddered for the final time and went limp. For Nonosabasut, time had stopped and the only thing he saw was his sister's face with the trickle of blood at the corners of her mouth.

One of Kirradittii's arrows embedded in the shooter's arm near the shoulder and he lost his grip on his hathemay. He turned and ran after his companion who had managed to push the tapaithook into the water. Tumbling into the boat, they frantically pushed it into deeper water. The one with two good arms paddled it toward the middle of the lake, as his companion, who was slumped at the back holding his bleeding arm, shouted encouragement.

Kirradittii launched three more arrows at the fleeing Indians, but only one reached them, piercing the side of the tapaithook behind the rower, just above the water line. When the Indians knew they were out of Kirradittii's range they stopped rowing and sat there shaking their fists, yelling something in their language at the two brothers glaring at them from the shore.

"Ignore them Kirradittii. They are no longer a threat and we can't reach them. We won this battle."

"But we lost our sister. They should all die. I wish we had a tapaithook."

"We have lost them all, brother. Our whole family is gone. There is only you and me."

"We have to go back and bury them."

Nonosabasut looked up at the sky. The afternoon sun was making brief appearances through the scuttling clouds. Out on the lake, the Indians had begun to row again and were now approaching the other shore.

Nonosabasut and Kirradittii walked to the two dead Indians and recovered their arrows and aaduth from their bodies. They then took the hathemays the Indians were carrying, snapped them in two and threw them into the lake.

"We will bury Tamarraa here and go back to the camp to take care of the others tomorrow. Then we will leave this place for good, said Nonosabasut."

"Yes," said Kirradittii. "This is no longer a good place."

Chapter 25
1795

For two long years, he and Kirradittii had wandered the cold northern coastline. Nothing had been the same after that fateful day when they had returned from the hunting trip and found their family had been violently taken from them. Life for both him and his brother had changed that day. Although they had been able to exact some small revenge, they were still left with an emptiness that they had not been able to fill.

They drifted from camp to camp, never staying long in one place. They travelled up and down the coastline, searching for a place that felt right for them. It seemed to Nonosabasut that was not to be. He had begun to think there was no such place, that their wanderings would never result in them finding a new home. Both him and his brother were fighting their demons of guilt and remorse at not being there for their family when they needed them most. He blamed himself for Tamarraa's death. He should have handled that better. She should still be here, but she wasn't and it was his fault. The picture of her reaching out her hand for him to save her as she lay there on the ground haunted him. In the past two years the memory had not faded. He feared it would be with him always.

Sometimes they talked of getting away from the coast, maybe moving into the interior. Kirradittii had been told of a large camp at the Great Lake. He had suggested they make the trip and see for themselves. Nonosabasut thought it would probably be good for them. Perhaps a change would make the bad memories go away. There did not seem to be anything for them here at the coast and things were getting less friendly as time went on.

They were finding that some of the camps they had previously visited were abandoned when they returned to them. Those that were not always had stories to tell; stories of the Buggishamen and how they were driving the Beothuk away and building their wooden houses where mamateeks had once stood; stories of the fire stick the Buggishamen carried that spat fire and could kill a man at a great distance. More and more often now, they encountered tribes who had to bury members of their families, killed by the Buggishamen. It was getting to be a dangerous place.

He and Kirradittii had not yet encountered the Buggishamen and were careful to avoid the coves where they had settled. Nonosabasut did not want to risk losing any more of his family so they were careful to stay away from them.

It seemed to Kirradittii that his brother had grown even more. He wondered when it was going to stop. He was head and shoulders over him, and although their wandering way of life over the last two years had made him leaner, he was still much heavier than him. His long unkempt hair hung down his back, almost to his waist, and a thick matted beard covered most of his face. He was an intimidating figure to look at and Kirradittii noticed whenever they entered a new camp that most people held back when meeting him for the first time.

Most of the anger that he had seen smoldering in his brother's eyes two years ago had gone but he had become more withdrawn and had not let go of the sorrow of the loss of their family. Kirradittii knew it was still there, under the surface, eating away at his brother. He knew he blamed himself for losing Tamarraa. He had heard him say so when he talked in his sleep.

Sitting on the other side of the crackling campfire, he shivered as he drew the threadbare blanket a little tighter around him. All around them the trees were covered with a thin layer of snow. It was always snowing here. The wind shifted the smoke and he squinted his eyes against the burn as it billowed over him. He looked through the swirling smoke at the huddled figure of his brother on the other side of the fire.

"Why don't we go farther south, Nonosabasut? Somewhere where it is warmer than this. It seems winter never ends here. I'm tired of it."

His brother just grunted. His head remained bowed.

Taking that as a maybe, Kirradittii continued. "You remember the place I was told about. The one they call The Great Lake. They say there are many Beothuk there. Maybe we should go see. We need to find somewhere to stay. This wandering around is no good. What is it we are looking for anyway?"

"Do you want a family, Kirradittii?"

Surprised at getting a response, Kirradittii hesitated a moment and then jumped in. "Someday I guess."

"Will you be able to protect them?"

"Yes, I will, but there is much to protect them from here at the coast."

Nonosabasut looked directly into his brother's eyes and nodded. Both understood what was unsaid, yet foremost in their minds.

"What about you, Nonosabasut? Do you want a family?"

"Yes, little brother. I do. I want many children and grandchildren to love in my old age. I don't want to wander around like this anymore. There is no point to it as you say, and we can't escape the memories anyway. Maybe we can go somewhere where we can make better memories."

"Then we should leave and go into the interior where there are many of our people. Where it is safer. Where we don't have to be looking over our shoulders all the time."

"Yes, you are right. Tomorrow we start travelling south. Let me get some sleep. I think I need to be around those that are young and still full of life," he mumbled.

In the distance, a moisamadrook howled and was answered by his hunting partners. Kirradittii looked up at the large round moon and the twinkling lights all around it. He tossed the remaining sticks on the fire, drew the blanket tighter, and curled up next to the warmth. He realized he was smiling in the darkness.

They followed the coastline for most of the morning. The sea was still filled with floating ice pans near the shoreline, and large icebergs dotted the horizon farther offshore. The bitterly cold wind sweeping in from the sea forced them to stay in the shelter of the treeline with blankets drawn tight around them as they walked. The weather seemed to be doing its best to reinforce last night's decision to move inland. They bowed their heads against the wind and silently trudged through the day, each with their own visions of what life might be like at the Great Lake.

At midday, they discovered a shallow cave, carved into the weathered rock by the unending motion of the sea, at the edge of a rocky beach. Grateful for the shelter, they crawled in out of the unrelenting wind. Although it was shallow, the wind did not reach them at the back, and it was a relief just to hear it whistling by the entrance. They sat with their backs against the rough rock wall and watched the sea fling itself against the rocks outside. Out in the bay, the wind tore spray from the tops of the whitecapped waves and whipped it into froth that now lined the water's edge along the beach. They quietly chewed on the dried meat they were carrying in their bags, thankful they were protected from the elements for a while.

"There is a small camp a little way down the coast from here," said Nonosabasut. "We should get there before dark. We will stay with them tonight."

"I remember it. There were only three families there when we came through before the snows started."

"It will be good to get out of this freezing cold for a night," said Nonosabasut, as he absent-mindedly picked up a rounded beach rock and rolled it between his fingers.

"It will," said Kirradittii, blowing on his hands to keep them warm, his words almost lost in the whistling wind at the mouth of the cave.

Nonosabasut tossed the stone through the entrance opening and watched as the wind pulled it away to the left and tumbled it along the beach.

"I guess it's time to go."

Reluctantly they stuffed the uneaten meat back into their bags, crawled back into the piercing cold, and began following the shoreline to the next cove. There they were forced back into the trees as they made their way over the tall cliffs that fell sharply away into the dark waters pounding the base far below.

Eventually the sheer cliffs gave way to flatter land and they once again walked the rocky beaches from cove to cove. As the afternoon wore on, the wind died down to where it was much more bearable, the bays were no longer covered in whitecaps, and the clouds overhead no longer raced across the sky.

As they walked through the sparse trees covering the point separating them from the next cove, Kirradittii looked over the broad shoulders of his brother and his face broke into a half smile, cracking his wind-dried lips, as he saw the telltale smoke in the distance. They were almost there. He ran his tongue over his lips to try and keep them wet, tasting the blood as he swallowed. He quickened his steps in anticipation of the warmth of those fires. He felt as if his very bones were frozen. There must be a better place than this, he thought.

Walking side by side with Nonosabasut, they had made it halfway around the cove when he noticed the figures on the beach ahead. There were two wooden boats pulled partially out of the water on the beach. He had seen them before. They were the kind used by the S'kiemoos. A small crowd had gathered near them and it seemed there was an argument in full swing.

Three Beothuk men were circled by eight S'kiemoos and several of the Beothuk women and children were standing on the outside of the circle. Amongst the group of men there was much shouting and waving of arms. Suddenly one of the S'kiemoos threw a punch and knocked one of the Beothuk on his back. Knives and hatchets were drawn and the battle broke out in earnest.

The Beothuk were clearly outnumbered. Nonosabasut and Kirradittii broke into a run and raced into the middle of the struggle, joined by some of the women as well.

All around them, bodies were locked in violent and bloody hand-to-hand combat. To Kirradittii's left, a young woman jumped on a S'kiemoo's back and pulled his fur hood over his face as her partner buried his knife into his chest, only to be dealt with a stunning blow from behind with a hatchet that opened his skull.

Out of the corner of his eye he saw two of them fall under his brother's powerful swings, and then he was locked into a death struggle with two of them himself. One was waving a knife back and forth in front of his face and the other was trying to circle around behind him. He bent and rushed the one holding the knife, grabbing his hand as they tumbled to the ground. Two of his fingers had come into contact with the blade of the knife and his hand was slippery with blood. Kirradittii rolled away to fend off the rush of his other attacker and one of the women hit the downed S'kiemoo with a large rock. He did not move again. His attacker changed direction and went for the woman.

Kneeling there on the loose beach rock, he looked over his shoulder in search of his brother. He was straddling another knife-wielding S'kiemoo who was lying on his back on the beach. Another one was sneaking up on him from behind with a hatchet raised over his head.

"Nonosabasut, watch out behind you," yelled Kirradittii.

Nonosabasut held the smaller man beneath him with one hand and half turned as the hatchet descended, catching him full in the face.

Kirradittii watched in horror as the hatchet sliced into his brother's lower face, spraying blood on the squirming S'kiemoo beneath him. Nonosabasut shuddered with the shock and his hand convulsed, snapping the wrist holding the knife. The S'kiemoo raised the hatchet to take a second swing and Kirradittii rushed him, plunging his knife all the way to its hilt in the middle of his back. The hatchet slipped from his hand as he shuddered and collapsed at Kirradittii's feet.

Kirradittii looked around him. His heart was pounding and his breath was coming in laboured gasps. The air he was drawing in through his nose was no longer the familiar salty sea air. It was tainted with the smells of death. But the battle was done. Three of the S'kiemoos were retreating to their boat, one of them limping and holding his open wounds. All around him lay bodies, dead and dying, moaning and crying in pain. His clothes were spattered in blood. Much of it was not his. He turned back to his brother who was lying on his back with his hands covering his lower face. Dark blood was dripping through his fingers. He was moaning softly.

Kirradittii dropped to his knees and leaned over him. Nonosabasut was breathing steadily but his eyes were glazed and he was mumbling something Kirradittii couldn't understand.

"You're alright, Nonosabasut. It's all over. What's left of them are gone. We need to get you back to one of the mamateeks. Can you stand?"

"Help me get him up," he said to one of the women standing nearby.

They managed to get him to his feet, draped an arm over each of their shoulders, and helped him walk up the beach to the nearest mamateek. Inside, they laid him on the ground and the woman left them to check the others at the beach.

Kirradittii dragged his brother closer to the fire and covered him with a caribou skin that was lying on the ground. Nonosabasut had stopped moving. Kirradittii bent close to his face and placed his hand on his chest. With relief, he felt slight movement. He guessed he had just passed out from the shock and pain.

Kirradittii checked Nonosabasut for other wounds but could find none. He sat back, wrapped a cloth around his bleeding fingers, and wiped the blood from his hand.

He then turned his attention to his brother's mangled face. It was almost too horrible to look at. The hatchet had done terrible damage, slicing his cheek on the right of his nose through the top lip and down to the bottom of his chin. The gash was deep, all the way to the bone in places, and a large piece of partially severed skin hung loosely over the side of his face. Kirradittii used water that was being warmed by the fire and washed out the wound. Gingerly, he maneuvered the loose skin back in place and sat back. He had no idea what else he could do. He wondered if his brother would make it and he swallowed hard against the burning lump in his throat.

The door to the mamateek was pushed aside and the woman returned with another of the women leaning heavily on her, followed by a young boy with blood on his hands and face.

"This is it," she said. "The rest of them are alright or dead."

"You have to help my brother. I don't know what to do for him."

"I will get to him as soon as these two are taken care of. Looks like you cleaned up the cut. That is good for now. I will sew it together later. Get this one cleaned up," she said, indicating the boy.

Kirradittii used more of the water to clean the blood from the boy's face and hands. It seemed most of the blood was not his, and he could only find some minor scratches. He was merely dazed from the battle he had just experienced.

"How many are dead?" he asked the woman who was working on the leg of the other one.

"Five of the S'kiemoos. We made sure of those," she spat out angrily. "They killed three of our men, two of the women, one of the older boys and my oldest girl."

"How many are left?"

"Counting you two, there are twelve of us. Besides the five of us here, there's the old man and his wife in the mamateek across the way, two more women, and three smaller children."

Kirradittii sat back on the ground. "What started this dispute?"

"I don't know. They started arguing over fish or something. This is terrible. They have wiped us out."

"Will they come back?"

"Maybe for their dead. I don't think there will be anymore trouble. We've dealt with them before. They've never been like this. They 've always been friendly."

"I think I'll drag their dead down to the point so they won't come near the camp. You come with me boy."

He slung his hathemay and a pouch of arrows over his shoulder and they walked down to the bloody battle site. Kirradittii stood there for a few minutes looking over the scene. All was quiet now, save for the harsh cries of the scavenging seagulls and the lapping waves washing up on the blood-stained rocky beach.

The surviving women had moved the fallen Beothuk up onto the snow-covered grass above the beach and were weeping quietly over the bodies as they prepared them for their final journey.

He looked out to sea where he could see the two boats in the distance. They had managed to launch both and had them tied together with a short rope. They seemed to be sitting there watching him.

"Let's get to it," he said to the boy. He slipped his hands through the arms of the nearest S'kiemoo and lifted his upper body. The boy took his legs and they carried him down to the point. They repeated this for the other four and laid them out in a row near the water.

The boats had not moved.

"What's your name, boy?"

"I am Spinnaatell."

"How old are you?"

"Twelve."

"Did you kill one of them?"

"I helped."

They walked in silence for a while.

"They killed my mother and father."

"I'm sorry. My mother and father and two sisters were killed two years ago."

"How?"

"Indians."

"Do you think the S'kiemoos will come back?"

Kirradittii looked out toward the boats. They were moving toward the shore.

"They are coming in," he said. "I think they will just pick up their dead, but we need to be ready. Can you shoot a hathemay?"

"Yes."

"Go and get it then."

They had reached the battle site and Kirradittii stood on the beach with an arrow notched while Spinnaatell ran to his mamateek to get his hathemay.

When Spinnaatell returned, they stood on the beach and watched as the S'kiemoos landed their boats and loaded their companions in the empty second boat. Once they had everyone in, they pushed off and rowed out and around the point without looking back.

Kirradittii watched them until they disappeared and then turned to go back to the mamateek. "Maybe you should go down to where you can see around the point to make sure they are gone," he said to the boy.

"I will."

"Come back and let me know what you see," he shouted at Spinnaatell's back as he ran down the beach toward the point.

Kirradittii turned and trudged back to the mamateek. He was worried about his brother. He knew he was strong but he didn't know if he would be strong enough to fight back from the terrible gash in his face.

Now he wished they had stayed out of the fight. They should have kept going to the Great Lake like they planned. Nonosabasut wouldn't be able to travel anytime soon, that was for sure.

Not only would they have to stay here, but he would have to do the hunting for this group. There was no one else.

He pushed open the door and stepped inside the mamateek. His brother was still not moving. The woman had made a strong-smelling paste that she had spread on the woman's leg as well as Nonosabasut's face, which she had sown together while he was away.

"It will help the healing process," she said, noticing Kirradittii's stare.

"What do you think his chances are?" he asked her.

"He is strong. He will live. He will never look the same, but he will live."

I hope you're right, thought Kirradittii. I can't lose any more family. He sat on the hard-packed ground next to his brother.

Spinnaatell pushed through the door. "They are gone," he said. "I watched them travel all the way around the next point."

For most of the summer Kirradittii sat by his brother's side, feeding him liquid meals, which was all he could eat for many weeks after the battle. The only time he left him was to hunt and gather food for the little group. Most of the time he hunted with Spinnaatell, who he quickly learned was an excellent shot with his hathemay.

He talked to Nonosabasut constantly, trying to distract him from the pain that often left him softly moaning. It wasn't until the cut began to heal that he could understand anything Nonosabasut was trying to say to him. Before then the words were thick and slurred, leaking through the holes in his face and chin.

Several weeks after the battle, infection set in the leg of the wounded woman. Three days later she was gone. Nonosabasut had been luckier. Infection had not laid a claim on him and his face was slowly healing. He was going to be left with one of the ugliest scars Kirradittii had ever seen, but he would live.

They had been joined by another family early in the summer, a couple with a twelve-year-old boy. That was a big help for Kirradittii. He no longer had to go on all the hunting trips. Spinnaatell and the new boy took care of some of those. It gave him more time to spend with Nonosabasut.

Kirradittii had not let go of the plan to go to the Great Lake and he kept reinforcing it to Nonosabasut whenever he could. Late in the summer they began to lay plans to make the trip as soon as the ice began to thaw, after the winter. They considered travelling during the winter but they had convinced everyone in the camp to accompany them and winter travel would be too difficult for some of them. So, they waited impatiently for the spring to come.

Once enough food had been gathered for the winter, Kirradittii set about training the two young boys in earnest. It was a long trip into the interior and they would need anyone who could use a hathemay to be trained. It was unlikely they would make such a long trip without encountering either the Buggishamen or the other Indians. They needed as many of the group prepared to defend themselves as possible.

Spinnaatell had already proved himself with the hathemay, so Kirradittii concentrated on the new boy. At first he set a single fixed target and had the boys practice until they were consistently hitting it, whether the wind was blowing or not. Then he moved on to multiple targets set at various distances. The boys were enthusiastic, and when Kirradittii turned it into a friendly competition their daily improvement was fun to watch.

By the time winter set in, Kirradittii was satisfied they were prepared and not only would make good hunters but would also be able to defend the group if it ever came to that. Now it was just a matter of waiting for the winter to end.

Chapter 26
1796

The long cold winter was just about at an end. The land was slowly shedding itself of the layers of accumulated snow and ice. Life and color would soon return to the land. The time had come to start the journey to the Great Lake. Finally, the wait was over.

The gash in Nonosabasut's face had healed into an angry red, raised scar. His old appetite had returned, he was eating normal food, and he could talk properly again. He was as anxious as Kirradittii to get away from the coast and find a safer place to live. He just wanted to leave this place and all its bad memories behind. He knew he would never come back once he left.

During the winter, while waiting to heal, he had fashioned a snow sled. It waited outside the mamateek door loaded up with everything it could carry. It too was ready to go.

The trip to the Great Lake would take a week, maybe more if the weather changed, and there was a big group so they would need a lot of supplies to get them there. The sled would carry most of the necessary things and they would hunt on the way for fresh meat.

The family that had joined them during the summer had been at The Great Lake before and knew the way. They would be their guides.

In total, there were fourteen of them. The only ones Nonosabasut worried about were the two older ones. They were not well nor strong like the rest and he wasn't sure they could even make such a long trip. He had talked with them and tried to discourage them, but they were firm and he had to respect their decision. They had lost their only son and daughter-in-law in the battle, so the only family they had were the other members of the small group. He wished they weren't going but it seemed there was no choice in the matter. They will probably slow us down some, but we'll get there, he thought, as he pulled the blanket up around him.

He was the first awake in the morning. The light of the day had not yet pushed back the early morning gray and he could still make out faint twinkling as he stared at the sky through the smoke-hole above him. He pushed back the blanket and dropped some small twigs on the ashes of last night's fire.

Stirring them with a stick, he uncovered a few embers. Gently blowing on them, he ignited a strip of birch rind and soon had flames hungrily wrapping themselves around the dry twigs. The soft glow of the fire, along with the snapping of the dry sticks, immediately transformed the inside of the mamateek, giving it the familiar feel of home. Won't feel this again for some time, thought Nonosabasut as he sat there enjoying the moment.

"Morning, Brother," came from behind him.

"Morning, Kirradittii," he replied.

"This is the day, Nonosabasut. We've dreamed of this for a long time. It's finally here."

"It is. We should get under way as soon as everyone has eaten. Sounds like a quiet day out there. Should be good for travelling."

"I'll go wake everyone," said Kirradittii as he yawned expansively and stretched his arms above his head.

The sun was over the horizon and climbing in the sky before everyone was ready to leave, but eventually they walked out of camp, leaving their homes behind. Nonosabasut and Kirradittii walked together, pulling the laden sled, behind the new family who was taking the lead. The old couple was placed in the middle and Spinnaatell and the new boy were at the back end of the strung-out column.

It was a good day to travel. There was still enough snow to drag the sled, but overhead the sky was completely clear and the morning sun took most of the chill out of the air.

They followed the coast for the first three days, skirting around two coves where the Buggishamen had built their wooden houses and wharfs. It added time to their journey, but Nonosabasut wanted to make sure they stayed hidden from the Buggishamen. They were a large group and left a well beaten path through the snow, so it was necessary to stay in the deeper woods to avoid contact. There was no reason to take the risk.

They didn't encounter any Beothuk until the morning of the fourth day. Last night they had camped at the mouth of a larger river. Tedamichaloo, who was leading them, informed Nonosabasut that this was the place where they would begin to travel cross country to reach the Great Lake by following a series of small rivers.

They quickly discovered the snow was deeper in the woods, just as it had been when they skirted around the Buggishamen settlements. It made it much harder going. For the most part, they had to break their own trail, sometimes wading through knee-high snow. It was getting much more difficult for the older couple to keep up and, to make things worse, the old man had come down with a severe winter cold.

By midmorning they reached a small camp on the banks of the river they were following. The smoke drifting lazily from the top of the three mamateeks was a welcome sight to them all, especially the old woman.

The children ran ahead and, by the time the rest reached the clearing, they were running and playing in the snow with the children of the camp. Their yells and screams as they raced around the snow-covered ground brought the adults out of the mamateeks. They stood quietly together and watched the small group of travellers' wade through the soft snow.

As soon as they reached the clearing, they were greeted with hugs and ushered into the mamateeks where warm food was quickly prepared and offered. Soon they were trading stories, and before they realized it the day had passed. They were invited to stay for the night and happily accepted.

Kirradittii noticed the looks some of them gave his brother, and one of the little girls hid behind her mother in fear when she saw the deep red scar running down his face. He wondered how his brother felt and was relieved when he heard him launch into the story of the battle and how he had gotten the scar from the S'kiemoos. As he often did, he absentmindedly rubbed the scar with his fingers as he talked.

Later that night when they had moved to one of the other mamateeks and he was alone with Nonosabasut, he raised the concerns he had with the old couple.

"I don't think we should take the old couple any farther, Nonosabasut."

"I agree Brother, but it really is their decision."

"I think it is too dangerous for them. The old man is getting sick. It is just making it too hard for the rest of us. You should try and convince them to stay here. I'm sure they would be welcome."

"I know Kirradittii, but would you say that if it was me that was still sick."

"It was our dream Nonosabasut. It was just supposed to be us."

"They are all part of our family now, Brother. That happened when we ran into the middle of their battle. That changed everything," he said as he idly rubbed his hand over the bumpy scar.

"Perhaps they will decide to stay here."

"Perhaps. I will talk with them in the morning."

"Tedamichaloo says we are about halfway there. It's been a good trip so far."

"At least the weather has been good."

"Let's hope it holds."

"This has been a long time coming, Brother. We will soon be there."

They left in the morning. The old couple were with them.

Kirradittii smiled at his brother. "I see you couldn't convince them to stay."

"It seems my words were not enough. They want to make it all the way."

It was slower going. They had to adjust for the pace of the old couple, but they were travelling through thicker forest with deeper snow so they wouldn't have been able to travel much faster without them. The trees were much taller here unlike the stunted trees of the coastline. This is much better country than up north thought Nonosabasut, must be something to see in the summer. I think life will be better here.

It was three days since they left the camp where Kirradittii had wanted the old couple to stay. The sled he was pulling was much lighter than when they had started. There was very little left on it, but that didn't worry him. They were almost at The Great Lake.

They were crossing the wind-swept ice of a large pond. At places, the ice seemed dark and thin. Kirradittii wondered if it was wise for so many of them to be walking together, so he dropped back from Nonosabasut and Tedamichaloo, who were in the lead, and slowed some of the people down to spread them out more.

Everyone except the old couple had safely reached the shoreline. Kirradittii stood on the bank and watched them trudge slowly toward him. The old woman was holding the old man's arm, supporting him over the more slippery places. Kirradittii smiled as he watched them. They had been together many years. Her love for her husband was plain to see by the way she fussed over him and supported him in his sickness. Kirradittii wondered if he would have someone like that someday.

The two of them were the last to cross the thin ice at the edge of the pond, and their combined weight was too much for the ice that had strained to support all those who had gone before. They were just a little way from the shoreline when, with a snap, the ice parted and they both slipped through into waist-high water.

Kirradittii pushed the sled across the gap. The woman regained her feet and pushed her husband toward safety. He grabbed the end of the sled and, with Kirradittii pulling and the woman pushing, they managed to get him ashore. They were both soaked with the icy cold water and collapsed on the bank, shivering violently.

They were quickly helped into the nearby woods and the men set about gathering boughs to build a shelter to protect them from the cold wind. A fire was soon going and they huddled near it, covered with all the spare blankets the group had.

Tedamichaloo and Nonosabasut were standing at the edge of the pond looking back the way they had come. It was mid-afternoon and it looked like they would have to stay here for the night. The air had gotten much colder and the wind was whistling ominously through the trees. Far in the distance, the sky had turned dark gray and there was no doubt a storm was chasing them down.

"How much farther, Tedamichaloo?" asked Nonosabasut.

"One more day's travel should do it."

"We will not be able to outrun that, will we?"

"No. Not if we have to stay here with them tonight."

"We don't have a choice. They will need to take some time after that fall. The old man was already sick. This is likely going to make him worse."

"Yes, we might as well make it as comfortable as we can for them and hopefully we can leave at first light."

By the time they were ready to leave in the morning, the storm had still not reached the camp, but much of the landscape behind them was blotted out by a thick blanket of swirling snow.

"We need to go now, said Nonosabasut to Kirradittii. "Get everyone up and on the move."

"We won't all be going," said Tedamichaloo from behind him.

"What do you mean?"

"They didn't make it."

"The old couple?"

"Yes. I checked on them. The cold was too much for them. They died sometime during the night."

"Are you sure they are gone?"

"Yes. She is still holding him."

"We have to leave them here for now. We can come back and take care of them when the storm passes. We need to get everyone moving before the snow hits."

A sense of urgency seemed to grip the group and they were moving out in a few minutes, following Tedamichaloo's lead.

Before long the storm caught them and the howling wind made it impossible for any communication. Nonosabasut and Kirradittii kept everyone moving through the day and by nightfall they were wading through waist-high snow. There was no where to shelter and, because Tedamichaloo felt they were close to the Great Lake, they pushed on through the night.

The smaller children were strapped to the sled and the adults pulled them through the storm. Kirradittii strung a rope between everyone in the group to keep them together, and he kept going up and down the line to make sure everyone was there. With their heads bowed against the blinding snow, they trudged along, trusting Tedamichaloo to get them to safety at The Great Lake.

Sometime after midnight they stumbled into the camp. The dark mamateeks appearing out of the night was the most welcome sight any of them had seen for many days.

They pushed their way into the closest ones and collectively collapsed on the floor in relief. Some of them barely felt the furs that were laid over them by the occupants. Overcome with exhaustion, they just fell into a deep sleep.

The next morning Nonosabasut opened his eyes to see Kirradittii pulling back the caribou skin that served as a door to the mamateek. Outside the wind had died and all was quiet. Through the partial opening, his eyes were met with a sun dazzled sea of white.

"We made it, Brother," he said with a grin.

"Yes, we did," said Kirradittii as he pushed through the piled-up snow in front of the door and crawled out into the brilliant sunshine.

The End

Author's Notes

This is the third and final book in the Red Indian series. Chronologically it fits before the other two and could be read as the first book. I, however, would suggest the series be read in the order they were written; *The Early Years, The Final Days,* and *In the Beginning*. This series was based on resources available, and although scanty, provided the foundation for these stories. I have taken liberties in fictionalizing the characters and incidents, but made the best attempt to keep them as close to history as I possibly could, although I must admit at times I found myself struggling to keep my imagination from running away with the story.

I hope this series will provoke a renewed desire to get to know these gentle people that one day long ago populated the beautiful island of Newfoundland, and in some small way, will serve to ensure their part in our culture and colorful history will never be forgotten.

Glossary of Terms

The following represents a list of Beothuk words used in this book. These were recorded by William Cormack during his many conversations with Shanawdithit.

Aaduth	*spear*
Buggishaman	*white man*
Gossett	*land of the dead*
Hathemay	*bow*
Moisamadrook	*wolf*
Monau	*seal*
Odemet	*red ochre*
Tapaithook	*canoe*
Wasemook	*salmon*
Washawet	*bear*

<u>Locations</u>

The Great Lake	*Red Indian Lake*
The Great River	*Exploits River*

Months of the Year

Kobshuneesamut	*January*
Kosthabonong bewajowite	*February*
Manamiss	*March*
Wasumaweeseek	*April, June and September*
Bedejamish bewajowite	*May*
Kowayaseek	*July*
Wadawhegh	*August*
Godabonyegh	*October*
Godabonyeesh	*November*
Odasweeteeshamut	*December*

Historical Characters

Several historical characters are represented in this book. As a work of historical fiction, fictional characters are used to develop a picture of the missing pieces and stories of what the lives of these historical characters might have been.

Terry's Books

Terry's Books

<u>*The Red Indian series:*</u>

Red Indian – The Early Years: published March 2015.

This, the first book in the series, follows the lives of Shanawdithit's mother, Shanadee, and her family as they struggle to survive the formidable challenges mounted against them by the arrival of the early European settlers to the shores of Newfoundland.

Red Indian – The Final Days: published March 2016.

The second book in the series brings the stories of the fifteen Beothuk that Shanawdithit reported to William Cormack were living at the time she was captured. It attempts to provide some insight into what may have happened to them as they disappeared.

Red Indian – The Beginning: published July 2017.

Having no access to pen and paper, the Beothuk passed on the stories of their families by word of mouth. The third book in this series records the stories of the ancestors of Shanadee and Kirradittii, as told so many times around the family campfire.

Bloody Point: published July 2019.

Legend has it that Hants Harbour, a small community on the eastern shore of the island of Newfoundland, was the scene of a terrible Beothuk massacre of unprecedented scale. Although history is vague on the facts, and the numbers may have possibly been exaggerated, there are those who still relate the story with conviction.

Beothuk Slaves: published October 2020.

Following a failed attempt in 1500, Portuguese explorer Gaspar Corte Real, landed on the island of Newfoundland. He captured fifty-seven Beothuk and sent them back to Portugal on two of his accompanying ships. Gaspar remained to further explore. He was never heard of again. This is how I imagine the end of his story.

Holmes: published July 2022.

Seasonal fishermen dared not venture to the southern side of Fogo Island for fear of an encounter with the Beothuk. That was before John Holmes. In 1823 he took the chance and set up tilts in Seldom Come By. Five years later he became its first permanent settler. This is his story. *Through Beothuk Land*: published July 2025

Through Beothuk Land: published July 2025

The year was 1822. The Beothuk population was now reduced to a few. William Epps Cormack launched an expedition to find any surviving members of the Beothuk nation. In his search, Cormack, with his young Mi'kmaq guide, walked across the interior of the island of Newfoundland. This book takes you along on this harrowing journey.

For information on Terry's published books as well as future books, please take a moment to "like" and follow Terry Foss Author Facebook page or visit Terry's website shown below.

Website: www.terryfoss.ca

Email: terryfoss@nf.sympatico.ca

Facebook: facebook.com/terryfossauthor

Distribution: www.shopdownhome.com

What readers are saying about Red Indian;

"Couldn't put the book away. Immediately, I was pulled into the life of this Beothuk family. The fiction and the facts were blended in a fashion that was realistic."

"Fabulous read, and well written captivating story. Great insight to part of our history that is heard of so little. I HIGHLY RECOMMEND it to all."

"A great piece of historical fiction that brings to life the tragic plight of the ill-fated Beothuk. Humanizes an often-forgotten people. Even though the ultimate ending of the book is known before reading, the story of each character draws you in and makes you care about their lives and deaths."

"Absolutely loved it! It was overall a great read. "

"I found it very sobering & exciting at the same time. Can still smell the smoke from their campfires and hear the wind flapping against their wigwams."

"This book is historical fiction but it reads like Terry was watching the characters from nearby and taking notes! It's a keeper for your Newfoundland Beothuk book collection."

www.ingramcontent.com/pod-product-compliance
Lightning Source LLC
Chambersburg PA
CBHW070556260626
47161CB00002B/619

* 9 7 8 0 9 9 4 0 2 0 9 4 9 *